Praise for the
novels of John Neufeld

Lisa, Bright and Dark

"Skillfully constructed and more exciting than Neufeld's previous, highly praised *Edgar Allan*."
—*Library Journal*

"Compassionate and tragic, an indictment of adults who refuse to get involved."
—*The New York Times*

"A surprise and a delight, despite its sobering theme."
—*Austin American-Statesman*

"John Neufeld has sharpened his pen considerably. . . . His young people may not be competent to deal with great problems, but at least they are willing to try."
—*The New York Times Book Review*

Edgar Allan

"Told with thoughtful simplicity . . . perceptive and convincingly drawn."
—*The Saturday Review*

"This is not a novel about prejudice or race relations or brotherhood or anything so simple. It is about parents and children, young people and older people, about love and failure, loss and discovery, coming to terms with oneself and others . . . a work of art."
—*The New York Times*

Lisa,
Bright and Dark

A NOVEL BY

John Neufeld

A SIGNET BOOK

SIGNET
Published by New American Library, a division of
Penguin Group (USA) Inc., 375 Hudson Street,
New York, New York 10014, USA
Penguin Group (Canada), 90 Eglinton Avenue East, Suite 700, Toronto,
Ontario M4P 2Y3, Canada (a division of Pearson Penguin Canada Inc.)
Penguin Books Ltd., 80 Strand, London WC2R 0RL, England
Penguin Ireland, 25 St. Stephen's Green, Dublin 2,
Ireland (a division of Penguin Books Ltd.)
Penguin Group (Australia), 250 Camberwell Road, Camberwell, Victoria 3124,
Australia (a division of Pearson Australia Group Pty. Ltd.)
Penguin Books India Pvt. Ltd., 11 Community Centre, Panchsheel Park,
New Delhi - 110 017, India
Penguin Group (NZ), cnr Airborne and Rosedale Roads, Albany,
Auckland 1310, New Zealand (a division of Pearson New Zealand Ltd.)
Penguin Books (South Africa) (Pty.) Ltd., 24 Sturdee Avenue,
Rosebank, Johannesburg 2196, South Africa

Penguin Books Ltd., Registered Offices:
80 Strand, London WC2R 0RL, England

Published by Signet, an imprint of New American Library, a division of
Penguin Group (USA) Inc. This is an authorized reprint of a hardcover
edition published by S. G. Phillips, Inc.

First Signet Printing, November 1970
60 59 58 57 56 55

Copyright © S. G. Phillips, Inc., 1969
All rights reserved

 REGISTERED TRADEMARK—MARCA REGISTRADA

Printed in the United States of America

For my father, without whose understanding and patience there would have been neither *Edgar Allan* nor this book

Acknowledgment:

My thanks to Dr. R. G., who works with "Lisas," and who worked with me to maintain psychological consistency.

And to others who so generously helped the manuscript develop: Jean Craig, Alice Miller, Ray Roberts, Jacqueline Weinstein, Robin Green, and to a former single lady saxophone player from Fort Worth.

* * * *

"Just make yourself comfortable and keep talking," M.N. said to Lisa. "Say anything that comes into your head."

But saying that to Lisa Shilling was like asking the ocean, as a favor, to turn cold in February.

For Lisa couldn't help saying anything that came into her head. On her good days, Lisa was as bright and natural as her friends; on her dark days, she was depressed, withdrawn, and deep in conversation with her "English voices."

Lisa Shilling, sixteen, was losing her mind.

M.N. Fickett, the first of Lisa's friends to realize Lisa's dangerous state of mind, is also the first to understand that Lisa's only hope of help must come from her friends. M.N. persuades Betsy Goodman and Elizabeth Frazer that "group therapy" is the answer—providing Lisa with a way of letting off some of the terrific inward pressure, postponing the inevitable explosion.

But Lisa doesn't make their work easy. She's alternately sensible and violent, open and deceitful, clear-headed and confused.

LISA, BRIGHT, AND DARK is a novel as current as the last time you looked at your wristwatch. Lisa and her friends are totally real, caring about real things: civil rights, sex, Paul Newman, riots, diet Jello, Paul Newman, and their futures.

Funny as young people are, concerned in the same way, determined but a little at sea, Lisa's "doctors" set out on a path of aid and comfort that will cause readers to reflect seriously, smile in recognition, and sympathize totally with Lisa and her illness.

* * * *

☆ 1 ☆

"Daddy, I think I'm going crazy."

Mary Nell looked up astonished.

"Oh?" Mr. Shilling said. "Why is that?"

"I can't tell you," Lisa said. "I just think it's true. And I'm frightened."

"More, Tracy?" Mrs. Shilling asked.

"No, thanks," Lisa's sister answered.

"Lisa?" her mother asked.

"No. Listen, didn't anyone hear what I just said?"

"We heard you, dear," Mrs. Shilling replied.

"What is it you're crazy about?" Lisa's father asked.

"Damn it, Daddy! That's not it at all." Lisa took a big breath, as though she were fighting something down.

"What is it, then?"

"That is it. I don't know. I only have a feeling that something is awfully wrong. Inside my head. I hear people. Talking, I mean, inside."

"Coffee, Mary Nell?" Mrs. Shilling offered.

9

"No, thanks, Mrs. Shilling," M.N. answered.

"Listen to me!" Lisa shouted.

Everyone did.

"I think I'm going crazy," Lisa said again. "I think I'm going out of my mind. Could we get some help or something?"

"Like what?" her mother asked. "You've mentioned this before, but you never say what you want to do about it."

M.N. was startled. This was the first time she'd ever heard Lisa say anything about this.

"Besides," Mrs. Shilling went on, "I think it's very rude of you to discuss this sort of thing when we have guests."

"Oh," M.N. smiled sheepishly, "don't mind me. Really."

"Since you don't pay any attention to me when we're alone," Lisa protested, "I thought you might with other people around."

"All right, all right," Mrs. Shilling sighed. "What is it you think you need?"

"Well," said Lisa, calmer, quiet but not hopeful, "maybe a psychiatrist or someone. I mean," she added quickly, "it wouldn't have to be an expensive one. Just someone who would understand and know what to do."

"You've seen too many movies," Mr. Shilling said.

"Who else has a psychiatrist, Lisa, in your class?" her mother wanted to know.

"How should I know?" Lisa said, clenching her teeth, trying to smile politely. "I don't

10

imagine it's the kind of thing people talk much about."

"I think it's exactly the kind of thing people do talk about, dear," said her mother, ringing a little silver dinner bell for the maid and smiling knowledgeably.

"Daddy, please," Lisa said, straining. *"Please, could you talk to someone, or get a doctor? Or maybe just do anything?"*

"All right, honey. As soon as I get back from Minneapolis," he said pleasantly and got up from the table.

Mary Nell said that Lisa just sat and stared at her father as he walked away. She started to turn toward her mother to say something but changed her mind. M.N. thought it might have been tears that stopped her.

And then Mary Nell saw Lisa's head begin to shake, ever so slightly. Not shake, exactly: quiver, up and down, from the chin. It was like palsy, M.N. said.

After a moment, Lisa too stood up and excused herself. Then she ran upstairs.

In her room, Lisa threw herself onto her bed and pulled up into a pony-position, on all fours, her sobs beginning the motion. Slowly at first, and then faster and faster, she began to rock back and forth, rhythmically smashing her head into the headboard.

M.N. stood in the hallway, listening through the door, before she eased it open.

11

★ 2 ★

My name is Betsy Goodman, and I count less
than almost anyone else in this whole story.

What that means is that I'm not overconfi-
dent about things. It's nothing like a huge
complex or anything; a lot of books say it's
common in people my age, which is fifteen.

I'm not what you could call ravishingly beautiful, except for my teeth. These, as my father
will be the first to tell you, are three thousand
dollars' perfect.

I'm about average height (five-four), and I
have dark, straight hair that falls to my shoulders without a hint of the slightest natural
curl. My eyes are big, brown, and near-sighted,
and when I absolutely have to I wear glasses.

Years ago my eye doctor told me that big,
beautiful eyes are almost always near-sighted.
It's the kind of well-meant statement that just
rolls around and rankles like crazy when you're
in front of a mirror looking into a horn-rimmed
face.

The only other thing that's even vaguely interesting about me is my ambition. I do not
want to be anything special—just what I think

I'd be good at: being married. Maybe with a couple of kids and a really groovy-looking husband, living on a beach in California, reading about other *special* people who wanted to be something more and were.

Right now, what I am is plain, single, and alive on Long Island (if you can stand it). But I am sort of simple which, when you find out more about some of the other people involved with Lisa Shilling, and about Lisa herself, is probably a very good thing.

To begin with, there's Mary Nell Fickett, who used to *live* in California! There are a few important things to know about M.N. fast: she's very, very smart (she'd like to be the first woman justice on the Supreme Court); her father's a minister, which has been madly helpful to us because he has a thousand and one books about everything you can imagine; and she's not at all like me.

She doesn't wear glasses; she looks like Shirley MacLaine; she has a great laugh and eyes that make you smile back without thinking. And she's fantastically popular with boys.

Sometimes I stand near her just to see how many and which of them will come up to talk. It's basking in her reflection, but it makes me feel a little prettier so it can't be all bad. Besides, psychologically, as long as I know the reasons for doing what I do, whatever I do is O.K. (that's a rough translation of something in one of M.N.'s father's books).

In spite of the fact that I'm younger than M.N. (I got a quicker start in nursery school, so

13

I wound up a little ahead of myself), she and I are friends. That means more than just living within a couple of blocks of each other. Like we talk on the phone a lot, go shopping together, and spend the night at each other's house every once in a while.

It's on those nights that I get my "lessons." M.N. thinks I need help in the boy department. I mean, if you examine my diary for the past year, you won't find it exactly bulging with gushy thoughts.

So M.N. spends a lot of time smartening me up. She arranges my hair and my wardrobe, and insists on hiding my glasses. *She* thinks I depend on them too much. *I* think I'm climbing the stairs standing still without them.

Naturally, we talk about everything in the world, from civil rights (which are M.N.'s big thing) to sex (which would be mine if I knew anything about it first-hand). And movie stars, and hippies, and free love, pot, potato pancakes, and Paul Newman; the Doors, censorship, Sly and the Family Stone. Strobe lights and see-throughs, Ethel and her kids, Paul Newman, Mia Farrow, the Iron Butterfly, and Paul Newman. Riots, Greenwich Village, suicide, San Francisco, diet jello, and Brian Morris.

He, if you want to know, is the cutest boy in our class. I mean it. He is absolutely gorgeous! The thing is, of course, he knows it. Still, zowee!!! M.N. likes to take him apart psychologically, examining everything he does for hidden motives and meanings. I just like to look at him.

Of course, he didn't belong to either one of us, then. He was Lisa's. At least, he was for a while before she went away.

If Mary Nell is the All-American Girl, and I nail down the All-American Schlepp spot, the role of Princess goes to Elizabeth Frazer.

Elizabeth is something else. For one thing, she has piles of loot. For another, she hardly seemed as though she were *in* our school at all. It was more like she was just visiting each day.

Which sounds dumb, I know. The reason for it is that Elizabeth is like Grace Kelly used to be: regal, cool, far off, blonde and slim, and with clothes you wouldn't believe. And intelligent.

M.N. is smart and studies. Elizabeth is *intelligent*. She never raises her hand in class, but if a teacher calls on her, she has the right answer as though it were something everyone automatically knew.

Furthermore, if you're suddenly missing a boy, look for Elizabeth, the flame among moths.

To be fair, though, the thing about her and boys was that she moved here maybe a year and a half ago. So, of course, being a new girl and all, *and* being beautiful and loaded, you had to forgive a lot and understand instead.

What Elizabeth Frazer had I hadn't (besides wealth, beauty, brains, and such) was confidence. By the ton. She never explained anything, and never made excuses. If she, E.

Frazer, did something, then of course it must have been right. At first, you thought she was unbelievably conceited. Later on, you didn't.

So there we all are, the three of us, with a sneaky look at Brian Morris (who just happens to look like Paul Newman, which certainly doesn't do any harm). What you don't have yet is a very complex, very simple—clever as can be but scarey as hell—sometimes cheerful and often so depressed you wanted to lock her up until the mood passed—girl named Lisa Shilling.

Lisa was crazy.

But not like "crazy, man!" I mean, out of her skull. Sick, psychologically. Insane.

We noticed something a few months ago. When *she* noticed it no one knew, but it was long before she tried to kill Elizabeth and, after that, herself.

☆ **3** ☆

We have a new high school in our town. It was exciting leaving our old dirty brick wreck with its broken windows, torn screens, no air-conditioning, broken hall lockers, and tuna fish sandwiches every Friday. Then we got to the new place.

It has green blackboards, indirect lighting, air-conditioning, a new gym, clean halls with lockers that really lock, an enormous cafeteria— and tuna fish sandwiches every Friday. I guess it doesn't matter how you wrap some packages.

School was where all of us met. It's where Lisa and Brian fell madly in love. It was perfect. Lisa was the kind of girl who couldn't have been called beautiful, really; everything just seemed to fit. She was alert and had a mean sense of humor, and she seemed more grown up than the rest of us. She had an air which said she'd seen more of the world than we had. She had great style, a marvelous but not too full figure, and fantastic legs—the kind of girl who is usually secretary of the student council, not because everyone who knows her likes her, but because it seems the office is hers by right.

This was great in the tenth grade, and even better in the eleventh, when Brian Morris got to be president of the council. This *was* unusual, because ordinarily the office goes to a senior. I think everyone just went wild over the idea of Brian and Lisa together that way. It happens, sometimes.

I really didn't know Lisa too well then (I still don't, honestly). She was Mary Nell's friend, not mine. I wasn't going steady or anything like that, and in our school people run pretty much in groups. I mean, if Brian and Lisa wanted to do something, they would do it with other couples, not with people like me. Mary Nell, at the time, had a thing going with

17

a senior almost as groovy as Brian himself. This one was a blond tennis player—the kind who goes to Yale or Princeton and winds up on Wall Street, joining lots of clubs. Anyway, that was how M.N. spent so much time with Lisa and Brian, and how I got to hear about everything they did.

Of course, there were a lot of things M.N. told me about I didn't pay much attention to. When one person always seems to be doing marvelous, groovy things, and all you get to do is hear about them, you can get a little depressed. So you learn to listen, or to seem to be listening, and to figure out when and how to nod at the right time, when to ask questions, when not to, and finally when to say you agree. This is called the art of conversation.

Or selective inattention, as my father says. Choosing what you want to hear and concentrating only on that. It was about six months ago that I began listening to Mary Nell when she talked about Lisa. Even being told about Lisa by a third person gave you the feeling she was undependable sometimes, a little strange.

The first thing I remember hearing was M.N.'s story about the night Lisa and Brian celebrated their first anniversary. A group of kids had gotten together for dinner and a movie, and then gone back to M.N.'s house. Lisa and Brian got funny presents, and there was dancing in Mr. Fickett's study. In the middle of the study, in the middle of the dancing, Lisa suddenly turned odd.

"Stop it!" she shouted, startling everyone.

"Just stop it!" Then she turned and ran out of the room.

M.N. and Brian followed, neither knowing what it was they were supposed to stop. Brian held M.N. back and went to Lisa in the living room. M.N., of course, stayed within earshot.

"What is it, honey?" Brian asked Lisa, putting his arm around her shoulders. Lisa stared at him without speaking. "What's the matter, Lisa?" Brian asked again. "What's wrong?"

After a minute, Lisa answered in a bitter voice. "You're no better than the rest of them," she said, cutting her words off so that she sounded almost English. "Why can't you all stop it, and leave me be?"

"But what have we done?" Brian asked.

"Oh, really," Lisa sighed as though she were suddenly very tired. "Why can't everyone mind his own business? Why can't people stare at something else for a change?"

Brian said nothing.

"Really, Brian," Lisa went on. "Your friends are about the rudest people I've ever known. I should just like to be left alone, if you don't mind."

M.N. walked into the living room then, and saw Lisa shake Brian's hand off her shoulder and turn away sharply, heading for an easy chair in a dark corner of the room. Brian watched her go, letting her settle into the chair. Then M.N. took Brian and led him back to the study, explaining that maybe it was "that time" or something and that Lisa was probably just a little depressed.

19

Which may have seemed true, for about ten minutes later Lisa was back with the crowd, dancing and laughing and her usual self. And that was that. I thought it sounded pretty weird, but I guess everyone (except M.N.) went back to normal, too, saying nothing more about it.

M.N. remembered her dinner at the Shilling's. She began to think that what she had thought was a great put-on might be real after all. She began to think about it, and then she began to talk about it, to me.

Which was fine, and it interested me like crazy, but it wasn't the best thing to do. For we both should have talked about it—to other people. We shouldn't have been so cautious and polite. We could have tried to do something for Lisa even then.

Hindsight, that's called.

★ 4 ★

Lisa next began to stay at home. She wouldn't go out with Brian if other people were going to be around. Even in school you got the feeling that she wished we would all disappear.

This was miserably hard on Brian. He and

Lisa were *the* couple in school: bright, popular, organized. They did things. He was captain of the hockey team. She was always at his side when he wanted her, helping and cheering or just standing there smiling with her arm through his. Before. Now, Brian found himself alone too much of the time.

He talked to M.N. about it, but she couldn't really do anything. Since Lisa hadn't mentioned illness to her again, M.N. decided she couldn't mention it to Brian. And although M.N. tried once or twice to get her to speak of her fears, Lisa said nothing. She still saw a few people in her room at home, but with the shades drawn and one tiny light on only. When she was in school, we began being able to tell when Lisa was having a black day, as we began to call them, and when she was having a fairly good bright day.

For she jumped from side to side for a while. Sometimes she would be her old self: confident, clever, open with everyone. Other times, she would withdraw, speak in a whisper, avoid meeting people in the hall or at lunch.

It got to the point where by her clothes you could tell her frame of mind. On good days, she was beautiful. She carried herself well and moved like an older woman who knew what moving one particular way could do to someone watching. On bad days, she wore dark clothing that only pointed out how pale she was, stooped over, with her shoulders hunched in toward her chest and her head down.

And all the time, Brian was going out of *his*

mind, naturally. He couldn't figure out what, if anything, he had done. What any of us had done, or what we were supposed to have been doing, which seemed more likely. Lisa decided she didn't even like going to hockey games with him. Then, when she would go, Brian was so nervous he played terribly. He never knew when she would decide to disappear, which she began doing a lot, or to suddenly arrive when he wasn't expecting her. He couldn't accept invitations to parties because he never knew whether Lisa would go with him and he didn't want to go alone, and he was afraid to find out what she would say if he did. It got so bad he once made a sort of pass at Mary Nell.

"It's absolutely true!" M.N. said. "He was just standing there, pawing the ground like an indecisive horse, and he asked me, just like that."

"Well," I said, "what did you say? Just tell me, for heaven's sake."

"I said no, of course. 'Oh Brian,' I said, 'Lisa is one of my best friends. I couldn't even think of going out with you. I'd die if she ever found out. Besides, her friendship means a lot to me.' "

"What did he say?"

"He said he knew I'd say that, but he couldn't think of anyone else to ask Lisa might not hate automatically."

"That's a point."

"Still and all," said M.N.

"What?"

"Well, it seems to me that if he really loved

22

Lisa, he would stand by. He could wait. It's not as though this can go on forever, is it?"

"If you're asking me," I said, "you've got the wrong person. I'm not even sure Lisa knows what's going on. Though I'm just guessing, of course."

"Yes, you are," M.N. reminded me. I didn't need reminding.

I felt very sorry for Brian. Especially so a few weeks later. M.N. told me he had broken up with Lisa. I suppose I should have felt sorry for her. After all, Brian Morris *is* the gasp!!!! in our class, and to lose him would kill any girl. But I felt worse for him than for Lisa.

I knew he hadn't wanted to stop seeing her. I guess maybe he felt he couldn't go on without having his own black days, and maybe even the same kind of trouble, whatever it was. It was something he knew he had to do, instinctively, even though it must have hurt very badly.

None of this touched Lisa. She came to school on good days and bad, and behaved accordingly. On good days she was cheerful and funny and would talk to M.N. about Brian as just a step in growing up, something that after all no one could expect to have lasted forever, and from which she had learned a great, great deal. On bad days, she said nothing to anyone, answering questions in class only with great effort and then almost inaudibly.

About this time I noticed something that M.N. hadn't. On her bad days, after she and Brian split, Lisa would walk from class to class with Elizabeth Frazer. Not with her, exactly, but at her side. She never spoke to Elizabeth, and Elizabeth hardly ever spoke to her. They just walked through the halls together, Elizabeth saying "hi" to people she knew and Lisa hiding behind her, saying nothing. As a matter of fact, it occurred to me that Elizabeth hardly even *looked* at Lisa as they walked. And if she spoke to her at all, Elizabeth did it out of the side of her mouth, as though the words were being slipped out secretly in case anyone were listening. It was sort of weird.

And then, one day, we got down to the nitty-gritty.

It was one of Lisa's good days. She had been happy all morning, and nearly brilliant in English class, using words even M.N. hadn't yet discovered. Her face, which is hard to picture because it can change so fast, was lit up, and her cheeks were flushed so that she looked like an Ivory Soap baby at sixteen—simple, clean, and unbelievably beautiful.

After English class, we all went to social sciences, which, I might say, is perhaps the major waste of our time each day. It was a day on which we were supposed to have (and did have) a test, so I rushed on alone to take a few last-minute looks at my notes.

After five minutes or so, everyone was in class and ready to begin except Lisa and Mary Nell. Our teacher passed out blue books and then fiddled around a minute, waiting for the two of them to show up. They didn't. So she passed out the test, face down, and held us up a minute more, still hoping to see Shilling and Fickett arrive.

"Betsy," she finally said, "you're near the door. Will you walk back and see what, if anything, is holding up those two girls?"

I stood up, frantically trying to find a way to grab my notes to cram with in the hall. No go.

It was natural to go back to where we'd been the hour before. I knew Mr. Milne had a break and wouldn't be around. So it stood to reason that M.N. and Lisa might still be in his room, fooling around and probably exchanging *their* notes at the last minute.

I opened Mr. Milne's door and looked in. I saw M.N. right away at Mr. Milne's desk, and I started to laugh. Mary Nell looked up at me, and I knew instantly I shouldn't.

M.N. had been bent over as I came in, with her head sort of under the desk altogether, doing something I couldn't see. When she heard me, she looked up terrified, and motioned me to be quiet. I was. Then I moved forward a little.

"Stop!" M.N. whispered hard. "Just don't come any closer!"

"What's going on?" I asked.

"Never mind," M.N. hissed. "Just get out of here and get the nurse, fast!"

"But what—"

"Will you please just do what I tell you!" M.N. nearly screamed.

Being curious and a little stubborn, I wasn't going to go until I knew what was happening. I walked on tiptoes up to Mr. Milne's desk and looked under it.

25

There was Lisa, on her hands and knees, doubled over, busily poking a pin into her wrist—neatly, rhythmically, precisely, watching tiny drops of blood peep out of each hole she punched. And M.N., bent down, not saying a word, kept handing her fresh pieces of tissue that Lisa took with a sort of smile to dab at the blood. She would put the tissue to the wound for a second, throw it behind her, and jab again with the pin. She didn't flinch. She didn't say "ouch!" or anything. Just huddled there, busy stabbing and staunching, stabbing and staunching, and M.N. powerless to do anything but watch and play her own awful part in the horrible thing.

I turned away and ran for the door.

★ 5 ★

This should have alerted everyone—the school, Lisa's parents (this time for real), and her friends. It didn't.

Adults—real ones—insist on thinking "soft." This process consists of looking on the bright side that, in most cases, is the dark one, saying that thus and so is only a phase. They feel there are some things from which "children" should be shielded. Adults are in many ways simply chicken: by protecting us, they protect themselves, which means that no one ever gets to the truth. This is not a good system.

That it isn't is what Lisa's story proves, I guess. For example, after Lisa had been bandaged and sent home, the school psychologist met with her teachers.

Our psychologist—"counselor" is another word we hear a lot—is a sweet old guy named Jeremy Bernstein. He's about fifty and wears glasses thicker than mine even. Mr. Bernstein means well. I'm certain of this. His problem is that he just doesn't know how to go about doing well.

He's a short man, shaped rather like a *C*, which surprised me a little because I've seen *C*-shaped people before but they're usually terribly tall. Mr. Bernstein isn't, but he's as self-conscious as if he were, which is why he's *C*-shaped, I guess. He's also very thin.

I suppose one reason Mr. Bernstein is self-conscious is because he can't see. And he's nervous about his job, which is dumb, because about the only people he ever sees are dropouts, or kids who are having difficulty staying in school even though they want to because of family reasons or something.

Other than this, all Mr. Bernstein has to do is a ritual sort of thing with every senior who wants to go to college. Each one is sent to his office for guidance counseling—picking a college. Mr. Bernstein smiles, tells each to sit down, and then asks what that person's first three

27

choices are and where to send the transcript of his grades. That's it. That's guidance.

So it wasn't unusual for Mr. Bernstein never to have run into Lisa Shilling before. What was unusual, I thought, was the way Lisa's breakdown, if I can call it that for a while, was diagnosed. After short conferences with all her teachers, Mr. Bernstein called Lisa's home and told her mother that Lisa was suffering from tension (ah-hah!) brought on by exams and by the fact that she and Brian were having some difficulty. He suggested that perhaps the Shillings should take Lisa out of school for a few weeks to rest, take her somewhere she could relax and think and pull herself together.

And that was that. No suggestion that anything was seriously wrong, or that poking yourself full of holes was anything rare in a sixteen-year-old girl who was supposed to have the world by the tail. (Who knew *what* the school nurse had reported, or to whom?)

Lisa's parents reacted the way we thought they would. They listened, sorted out what they wanted to hear—that Lisa needed a rest—and sent her off to Florida for six weeks. Alone.

Now, Lisa's parents are, on the surface, phonies. I can't talk about their insides. Mr. Shilling is a terribly busy man, always leaping around the countryside in his job, talking big and being maybe big and looking like an older James Fox. He's as good looking as Brian Morris is but with one difference: Mr. Shilling is flashy. He tries too hard to be clever, too hard to be quick, too hard at everything except at being himself. I'm not sure, after all these years, he could even remember what "himself" is.

He's the kind of man who looks great, but every time he stops before a mirror you hear him mentally writing a caption beneath the picture he "sees" in *The Times*: "*Mr. Shilling shops at the better shops; among his favorites are Tripler's, Neiman-Marcus, and Brooks'.*"

In other words, caught by cold hard cash. His wife doesn't help much to soften him. She's about forty with a good enough figure and abominable taste in clothes. I can't describe them because you wouldn't believe it. Maybe it's enough to say she looks like Shelley Winters playing a roadhouse pick-up (I happen to like Shelley Winters; it's the look I can't stand): stretch-pants two sizes too small, preshrunk sweaters with classic midriff bulge, a fur coat slung over her shoulders, and a scarf hiding the curlers in her hair.

Mrs. Shilling is tough clear through. It won't come as any surprise to find out that she and her husband pay almost no attention to Lisa or to Lisa's sister, Tracy. The one detail that sums this lady up is that she lives in an enormously expensive house with two living rooms—one all in soft pink (curtains, carpets, furniture), which no one is allowed to enter without first taking off his shoes and which, in fact, seems never to be used; the other, which has been, is so uncomfortable there isn't one chair in the entire room into which you can sink and feel at ease.

Mrs. Shilling also talks funny, in a way she

must have copied from the movies—through her teeth, with her lips tight and her mouth hardly moving. It's what, out here on the Island, we call "Locust Valley Lockjaw," and it's supposed to belong only to the very rich and the very snooty. Mrs. Shilling tries hard to be both.

Everything that Lisa's parents wish they were, and pretend to be, Elizabeth Frazer's really are. Mr. Frazer is a quiet, distinguished-looking man about sixty who has real style. His clothes may come from the same stores as Mr. Shilling's do, but on him they look different. Better, of course, and in character. Mr. Frazer can talk with you and make you feel instantly at home. He reminds me of something I read about Franklin Roosevelt, I think it was. That he knew a little something about everything in order to make conversation pleasant for anyone he met. It's a great thing, and I admire Mr. Frazer for it.

Mrs. Frazer, too, is truly interested in what we're doing. The only difference is that she seems busier than Mr. Frazer. The Frazers have an apartment in New York as well as their big house in our town, and Mrs. Frazer's attention seems broken into two pieces like her homes. You can be listening to her talk about one thing and then, without your being aware of the shift, she's talking about something else at the same speed. It's a little unnerving. Still, she is a lady and she went to Smith, which is where I would like to go but where I'll probably never even see a blade of grass. We just haven't got

30

that kind of cash, one, and two, I suspect I'm not that smart.

I can't complain though, for in some ways I guess I'm the luckiest of us four. My father is an insurance salesman. He has always been one, and I don't think it bothers him that he always will be. He makes a good living, good enough, he says, to take care of his family as they should be, and to have a little fun when we can. He's about medium height and looks about medium in every respect. I like him and I think he likes me. As a person, I mean, not just as his daughter. This matters a lot to me. It means we can talk when we have to, and be calm and look at things realistically.

My mother, of course, would like Daddy to want to be something more than he is. But she doesn't complain with any real strength. She adores him. Although she rules the house when he's in town during the day, she's quick to turn it back over to him when he comes home each night. Not that she's weak at all. It's just that she feels she has so many other things to do.

And she has. My mother is a joiner. She's always been homeroom mother either for my sister (who's four years older than I am and left college to marry a really sweet guy) or for my class or for my brother Ben's. She's on P.T.A. committees, on a Planned Parenthood board of some kind, is neighborhood captain or chief or whatever of the Cancer Fund. This, plus raising the three of us and keeping Daddy happy. There is less time for talk with Mother than with my father, but when something is really important

31

she stops, takes a breath, sits down wishing like mad for a cigarette (she gave them up a year ago), and then gives you her undivided attention and advice.

Advice is something Mary Nell's father gives, too, but it's not always easy to understand. The Reverend Mr. Fickett is a handsome man, but you get the feeling he's not as strong as you would like a minister to be. He's always enthusiastic, but then he has to stop to be practical. He's better at being enthusiastic.

Mary Nell's mother is a dream. She's had four kids and at the same time has always had to be mother to a whole community. Mrs. Fickett is very tall, and gray, and looks like what my idea of an old-fashioned New England first lady must have looked like. She's thin, with very strong features, and has a way of talking to you that really makes you feel like the most interesting person in the world. Her bright blue eyes sparkle, her mouth turns up in a smile that lasts as long as it should and no more, and her questions and interest aren't pretended. I like her a lot. . .

And now I'll tell you something terrible. While Lisa was away M.N. and I began to doubt. We began to think that maybe Mr. Bernstein and the Shillings *did* know what they were doing. That maybe all Lisa needed *was* a rest and a chance to think, time to discover that what was bugging her was just that— something that was simply bugging her and not at all as serious as she had imagined.

I guess this was because we were still younger

than those people and, for all our determination and sympathy, still unsure. But it embarrasses me now to think about it, just the same. Because when Lisa came back, you could see at first glance that her trip wasn't all she had needed. It wasn't what she needed at all.

☆ **6** ★

Lisa's first day back at school was difficult for everyone. Teachers treated her tentatively, as though they were afraid she might go off the deep end any minute. We—us kids—weren't sure what to do either, except pretend nothing had happened and wait for Lisa to give us the lead.

On the surface, Lisa looked well. Her eyes were unbelievably clear, her face tanned, and she seemed calm.

If you looked a second time, or looked the first time more closely, you could see underneath the calm. The eyes were clear, but wild, close to hysteria. Her voice was louder than before and her speech was faster, as though by being both loud and fast she were drowning out something the rest of us couldn't hear.

She dressed as she had on her good days, before she went away, and told everyone she

33

met that they, too, should have a little break-down of their own, just to be able to sit at the water's edge and catch the rays.

After school, to M.N., Lisa said something different. The place her parents had sent her had been, really, a rest home. (I admit, when M.N. told me this, I was a little annoyed. But only because I think of the Shillings as first-rate villains who never have positive thoughts about Lisa at all.) They had phoned ahead and spoken to a resident doctor. But they hadn't told him about the scene under Mr. Milne's desk, or about the blood and the stupidity of it, just about Lisa's "tension" and need for a change of scene.

So, when she arrived, and after some weird sort of entrance exam or interview or whatever, Lisa was ignored by one and all. Worse, the other patients were all old people. There was no one to talk with, no one to talk to, no one to help *her* at all. The place let her do as she pleased, gave her three decent meals a day, and let her alone. For the six weeks she was there, Lisa got up each morning, walked out onto a pier, sat down, and looked at the water looking back at her. Nothing more. She hadn't a thought in her head, she told M.N., except maybe one: that she *was* going bats, that she really was out of her mind.

M.N. said that Lisa said this with a laugh. That obviously it wasn't true, as anyone could see. I wasn't sure. It had already occurred to me that Lisa's brightness in school that day was sham. That she must have decided that crazy was what she was and, having given fair warning, she would enjoy it.

But for the first few days after her return everything seemed pretty much as it had been before. Even Brian was attentive. He walked Lisa through the halls between classes, took her to a movie and dinner, and it seemed as though they might, after all, get back together again. We all thought this would be a good thing.

But then things changed. Lisa came to school one morning dressed for a dark day. She spoke to no one and ate lunch alone, ignoring one and all, rebuffing anyone who tried to talk to her. Brian took one look and never looked again.

M.N., with her usual look-on-the-bright-side-manner, decided that this was only a temporary mood, almost a kind of joke. Lisa had been gone so long her teachers had decided to let her continue her courses without make-ups. With that problem out of the way, there shouldn't have been any "tension" since *she* had said she could live perfectly well without Brian. There was no reason for her to be "that way" more than a day or two, M.N. said. I decided, though I didn't say so, that the phrase of M.N.'s, "no reason at all," was exactly right. It was not reassuring. For, by this time, though I had never been one of her close friends, I was truly worried for Lisa.

Things got worse instead of better. Lisa slipped back into her dark days' mood altogether. She would answer her teachers' questions but only in a whisper. Once, when she was

35

called on in calculus, Lisa looked around guiltily and seemed to shrink before she got up from her desk. Then—as though hiding from everything in the world—she tiptoed to Miss Strane's desk and whispered, *in her ear,* the answer to the question!

It was hard enough watching, and harder still for most people to watch without laughing or making fun. But what happened was that everyone in the class that day realized that something really was wrong with Lisa Shilling. So she was allowed to behave as she wished, without snickering or catcalls or cruelty.

For most of Lisa's classmates were sympathetic. The word was out. People were as careful as they could be around her. We tried our best to adjust to her so as not to jar her any more than was necessary. We ignored her when she seemed to want this, and when she wanted friends, we were available. In other words, we were scared to death of what was happening in front of our eyes. We didn't need to know why it was happening. It *was* happening, and it needn't have happened to Lisa alone. It could have happened to any of us.

What did make me mad, though, was that the school staff was also scared. I know one isn't supposed to seek a double standard of behavior, but I still got mad when I thought of it. Naturally, you couldn't count on Bernstein to do much. But Lisa's other teachers could have done something, even if only telephoning the Shillings. Instead, they too seemed to want to believe that Lisa's behavior was "normal" and nothing about which to be alarmed. Maybe they thought, as we had, that Lisa was putting the whole school on. But after a while you could see this wasn't true. You just wondered what she would do next.

The only person I know who wasn't afraid of Lisa was Elizabeth Frazer. For some reason, Lisa had again drifted in Elizabeth's direction and used her in an odd way, as a shield from the rest of us. And Elizabeth still didn't talk to her, or seem to pay her any mind at all.

One day, as M.N. and I were walking home from school, she stopped short, grabbed my arm, and looked at me happily. "That's it!" she said. "We'll just have to do it!"

"What?" I asked.

"Help Lisa ourselves, of course. Obviously no one else is going to. Her parents don't believe anything is wrong. Most of the teachers are chicken. *We* can't set Lisa up with doctors."

"How are we going to help, then? You don't even talk to her anymore. She won't let you," I said.

"I know, I know," M.N. agreed. "Still, we ought to be able to turn somewhere for help. And you'll have to be in on it."

"Me! I hardly know her. She doesn't even recognize me most of the time. She's your friend, not mine."

"Well," M.N. said, "that may be true. But you're *my* friend. You'll just have to help *me* help her."

That kind of reasoning is hard to beat. So I stood there, waiting.

37

"We have to convince Lisa's family that she's in real danger," M.N. said after a moment. "We'll go to her house and tell her parents what's happening in school, and that Lisa wasn't kidding, after all. They can't help but be upset and they'll have to get some professional help for her."

"Mr. and Mrs. Shilling?" I said. "They won't even admit there's anything odd going on."

"They will if I can get to them," M.N. answered. "And, just in case they don't, while I'm at their house you can talk to Mr. Bernstein. *He'll* make them see."

"Bernstein! You've got to be kidding! He's about as forceful as Prissy in *Gone with the Wind.*"

"Well, anyway, as a back-up, just in case the Shillings don't understand me, they might understand him. You'll just have to do it."

"What on earth am I going to say to the man? That Lisa's ready to be committed? He won't believe me. I'm not even certain myself that it's true."

"What," said M.N. in her coldest voice, "exactly would convince you? Another session under Mr. Milne's desk?"

I shivered. "All right," I said. "All right. I just don't know what I'll say is all."

"Neither do I, to her parents. But it's got to be said, just the same, whatever it is."

And that was the beginning of the Fickett-Frazer-Goodman Psychiatric Clinic. Barely the beginning.

☆ 7 ★

The next day, as soon as school was out, Mary
Nell got Brian to drive her to the Shillings'
house while I went looking for Mr. Bernstein.
M.N. wanted to get to Lisa's mother before
Lisa herself came home from school.

I dawdled a bit since I still wasn't sure what
I was supposed to tell Mr. Bernstein. About
ten minutes after the final bell, though, I was
standing outside his door when he himself appeared, on his way home.

"Oh," I said, backing away a little.

"May I help you?" Mr. Bernstein asked. He
stood in the doorway and looked at me with a
funny little smile. Hopeful, I supposed. "Is
there something I can do for you?"

I tried to smile back. "Yes, sir," I said. "I was
wondering if I could talk to you for a minute or
so?"

"Ah, yes," Mr. Bernstein said and retreated
into his office, motioning me to follow. I did and
he closed the door as I sat down.

Mr. Bernstein's office was hardly more than a
large janitorial closet, which I guess pretty well
indicates how high he was held in the estima-

39

tion of the school. Perhaps it was a state law, I thought to myself, that each school had to have a guidance counselor or whatever, for obviously no one thought too much about it. I had the feeling I was one of the few people who had ever walked into Mr. Bernstein's office without having been sent there.

"Now then," he said, "I don't know who you are, do I?"

"My name is Betsy Goodman. But it's not because of myself I came," I said fast.

"Oh? Who then?"

"Lisa Shilling."

"Miss Shilling," he sort of whispered and stopped smiling. He leaned back in his chair and swung back and forth in it in very small arcs for a few seconds. "What is it, then, that you want?"

"Mr. Bernstein, she needs help. Real help, more than you probably have time to give her," I said, congratulating myself for tact.

"Why?" Mr. Bernstein asked. "She's had a good rest. Didn't she come back beautiful and rested? What more does she need?"

"More than *that*," I said, not really sure what it was Lisa did need. "I think she really *is* going out of her mind and nothing here can stop it."

"What is it you want to do?"

"Well, I—*you* have to impress her parents with how sick she really is. You have to make them see she's in real trouble and needs ... needs some kind of treatment. Maybe even a full-time psychiatrist or something."

40

"I don't think they want to listen to anyone," Mr. Bernstein said. "I have the feeling that the Shillings don't want to know anything about sickness. Even in their daughter. Besides, I'll tell you something. They wouldn't listen to me, even if I called them."

"But why not?"

"My dear Miss Goodman, are you old enough to understand something? No one likes to have their lives intruded upon. If I call, they'll think I'm criticizing the way they raise their children. And I would have to give them good reasons for interfering."

"Well, there you are!" I said. "If you have to give them reasons to convince them something is dreadfully wrong, then you just tell them what's been happening. None of us cares whatever else you tell them, as long as it works."

"*They* would care," Mr. Bernstein said, suddenly very quiet. "They would care, indeed they would. And they would care it was me who called them."

Mr. Bernstein sat motionless for a moment, turned away from me and looking up at the ceiling, said again softly, "They would care it was me."

For a minute I was stopped. But then I decided this was no time to reassure Mr. Bernstein that not everyone worried about life in the same ways he did. So I leaped in another direction instead. "Well, then," I said brightly, "maybe the way to do this is to tell Mr. Jackson. They would certainly listen to the principal."

41

Mr. Bernstein swung around to face me. "I don't think that's a very good idea," he said.

"But why? If you can—"

"Because it could be misinterpreted, Miss Goodman. If Mr. Jackson knew and did anything, it would seem as though it were a disciplinary problem. And you *know* the Shillings wouldn't buy that. Besides," he said thoughtfully, "that isn't the case. I've heard about this girl again from her teachers. And I think you're right. It wasn't just examinations or that boy. It is different, worse, deeper. But I have to find better reasons, and that isn't easy without talking to Miss Shilling herself."

"Then we'll persuade her to see you," I said quickly.

But Mr. Bernstein got nervous all over again and began his little swinging motion in his chair. "No, no. I don't think so," he said quickly, under his breath. "No, not yet." He turned around in his chair and looked at me without blinking, deciding, I guessed, whether to be honest or not. "I promise you that if I find a way to do something, I'll do it. But you must not depend on me." He looked very sad. "You must not depend on me."

I was still a moment, and I think I was staring. I couldn't believe him. Sitting there, swinging, he just announced he was of no use, no value, and he wanted *me* to understand!

"So," Mr. Bernstein said suddenly, smiling now, "we'll look into this together, then." He stood up. "I'm glad you came to see me, Miss

Goodman. We'll certainly look into this. O.K.? O.K." He was relieved.

I stood up, too. "O.K., Mr. Bernstein," I said quietly. "O.K.," and then I turned to leave.

"Miss Goodman?" Mr. Bernstein called. I stopped and turned around again. "Miss Goodman," he said, "try to see. Try, yes?"

"Yes, Mr. Bernstein," I said. "I see."

That evening after supper, M.N. and I met at her house. I was dying to find out what, if anything, had happened at the Shillings'.

"Nothing," Mary Nell said.

"Nothing? What do you mean? Something must have happened."

"Not really. I never got any farther than the kitchen."

"The kitchen?"

"The kitchen. I got there and rang the front doorbell. Mrs. Shilling came and looked through the curtains. Seeing it was only me, she motioned me to go around to the back. So I did. She was kind enough to let me stand just inside the backdoor, on a doormat, for the next few minutes."

"That's ridiculous!"

"True," M.N. agreed. "In fact, you have just summed up Mrs. Shilling's reactions altogether."

"She didn't believe anything?" I asked.

"Nothing. Yes, she knew Lisa was a little on edge. Lisa had told her herself that—"

"On edge! She's already in midair!"

"You know that, I know that, and Lisa knows that. Mrs. Shilling doesn't," M.N. said.

"Furthermore, she didn't appreciate the fact that I, a presumptuous sixteen-year-old child, should come to tell her about her own family and how to run it, thank you very much."

"Well, that's certainly plain enough," I said.

"Mrs. Shilling is nothing if not a plain-spoken woman," M.N. said with a mean sort of smile. "Anyway, she knows her family well enough to take care of it, she said. Hadn't she just spent God knows how much money sending Lisa away for six whole weeks to do nothing but laze around in the sun dreaming?"

"It's not as though she couldn't afford it," I said.

"I said that, too. I couldn't help myself. That's when I was shown off the doormat and into the driveway," M.N. said with a shrug afterward. "You know, I feel sort of like Chicken Little. What the hell would have happened if the sky really had fallen in?"

"What do we do now?" I asked.

"We wait here for Lisa. She said she would come by in a little while. I decided to ask her over so we could tell her we know and understand, and that we want to help."

"Do you really think she'll come? Or listen?"

"I don't honestly know," M.N. admitted. "I just hope so."

So we had our first session with our clinic's one and only patient, Lisa Shilling.

For Lisa did show up that night. Maybe it was out of loyalty to Mary Nell. Perhaps it was only to escape her own family for a few hours. Or maybe it was because she knew how dangerously close she was to hitting the bottom of the gulch. Lisa is a very smart girl, if I didn't mention it before.

Anyway, she arrived looking worse than we had ever seen her because she came at night. The bell rang and M.N. ran to get it. She opened the door and gasped, for Lisa seemed as though she had come from another world. Her clothing was entirely black, and she had make-up on we had never seen before—dark lines beneath her eyes, and coal-black above them, which made her eyes seem to be six inches back in her head. The whole effect made her face longer, paler, and just plain scarey.

I stepped forward as quickly as I could while M.N. was recovering, because we had decided it was important to get Lisa into the house without being seen by any of the Ficketts, parents

45

or kids. I took Lisa's arm and led her into the Reverend's study, closing the door behind us as fast and as quietly as I could.

Lisa was motioned into a chair while M.N. and I sat side by side on the couch facing her. M.N. didn't speak right away. She couldn't take her eyes off Lisa. This wasn't the best thing in the world for her to do.

"Do you mind!" Lisa said quietly but sharply.

"Oh!" M.N. said. "I am sorry, really. There's no reason, I suppose."

Lisa nodded and swung her swivel chair around to the bookshelves behind her. M.N. looked at me, pleading for me to help but I didn't. At least not right away. After all, this was M.N.'s idea, her party.

"You certainly know how to make a person feel at home," Lisa said suddenly, still looking up at the bookshelves. "Here's one of my favorites. *Principles of Abnormal Psychology*, by Maslow and Mittelmann. It's an absolute knockout of a book." Then she swung around to face us, straight on. M.N. coughed.

I couldn't help myself. "Lisa," I said, "we believe you."

"What do you believe?" she asked me haughtily.

"That you really are ill," I said. "That it's not just a temporary thing, or a phase or anything."

"Yes," said Mary Nell finally. "Yes, that's right. We know."

"Well?" Lisa asked.

46

"Well," M.N. said, at a loss. "We want to help somehow, if we can. How can we?"

"How can you indeed," Lisa echoed. "How can anyone?"

"But there must be something to do," I said. "We know you're not going to get help from your family. M.N. went there this afternoon and tried to talk to your mother about it."

"You did?" Lisa said, for the first time showing some interest. Her voice softened a little. "I could have told you," she said, mimicking her mother and speaking through locked jaws, "if you had asked, that you wouldn't get anywhere that way."

I smiled at her. "We thought it was worth a try."

"That's right," Mary Nell said, sounding a little stronger. "And while I was with your mother, Betsy went to talk to Mr. Bernstein."

"And?" Lisa asked.

"Nothing," I replied.

"He's a nice man, though," Lisa said. "I feel sorry for him."

"So do I," I said, "but that doesn't do us much good."

"What will?" Lisa wanted to know. "Listen, I've *tried* to talk to my family. M.N. was there once. *She* knows. They think I just want to do something everyone else is doing. That's a laugh! I'd love a little company! They won't pay any attention to me until I'm in some violent ward on a third floor behind bars."

"But you can't give up!" M.N. protested. "There must be something to do."

47

"Well, what were you thinking of when you asked me over?" Lisa asked.

M.N. hesitated. "I guess it sounds a little funny," she said, "but I—we thought that by letting you know we cared, that we were worried and didn't want to lose you—we thought we could work together on it."

"How?"

"Well, nuts, Lisa!" M.N. said. "You're not making this very easy."

"It wouldn't be easy in any case, darling," Lisa said with a sad smile. "No matter what *you* decide to do, *I* won't be able to help you very much."

"All right, then," M.N. said, thinking about this for a second. "All right. Lisa, what we thought of doing was trying to help you ourselves. A kind of group therapy thing, where we could talk and try to learn and understand, and maybe beat whatever the thing is."

This was news to me! M.N. was winging it! The minute I heard her idea I knew she needed support. And as I spoke, I began to think she might be on the right track after all. "What we hoped was," I said, "that by knowing we cared and were concerned, you could talk to us about it and take some of the pressure off. It would give you a way of getting away from it, of looking at it and trying to figure out exactly what's going on and what is going to go on." *God bless M.N.*, I said to myself.

"Betsy," Lisa said, *"that's* what scares me the most. I already know what's happened. What I don't know is what's coming next. I

48

can't turn anything off. I tried to, in Florida. But now it's here and almost comfortable, if you know what I mean. Familiar. I even like it a little, though it scares me. About the only thing I can think to do is sink into it. Sink in and let them take me away when the time comes." She said this without bitterness, without fear, like a weather report on the telephone: flat, emotionless, distant.

"That's exactly what we meant," I said. "You see, you *can* talk to us about it. Wouldn't that be *any* help?"

"It might be," Lisa said. "I don't know."

"And I think if we ask him again, Mr. Bernstein will help a little, too. As long as he doesn't have to get involved personally," I said. "You know, he's very insecure about some things, and he's worried about——"

"Part of the answer is here," Lisa said out of nowhere in an out-of-nowhere English voice I hadn't heard before. It was cold and deep and new to me.

"What?" M.N. asked quickly. "What did you say?"

Lisa looked at us a moment. "There is, actually, one person who might understand," she said, nodding to herself a little as she spoke in her new voice. "There is just one who might very well know."

"Who?" I asked. "Tell us."

"Frazer," Lisa answered, standing up. "Elizabeth Frazer, actually."

"But why her?" M.N. demanded.

Lisa looked at M.N., smiling coolly. Then she

49

walked out of the study, down the hall, and out into the night and the darkness and the world of soft pink living rooms.

★ 9 ★

We closed the study door and stared at each other.

"M.N.," I said, "*that* was the supreme clutch play of all time."

"What are you talking about?"

"That group therapy business," I said.

"Have you got a better idea?" M.N. asked sharply. "Besides, it just might work."

I smiled as warmly as I could. "It just might."

"So," M.N. said, "what now?"

"You're the resident genius. My only question is did Lisa say she would let us help or not?"

"She didn't say we couldn't, so we'll assume she meant we could. And we may as well begin now, since we're here together."

She stood up and went to the wall of books behind her father's desk. "The first thing," she said, "is to write down what we know so far

50

about Lisa's symptoms. The second is to try to match them here, in Father's books."

"I meant to ask you," I said, "how come your father has all these screwy things, anyway?"

"Well, he's on the front lines, after all," M.N. said. "I mean, he sometimes runs into people who are disturbed. If he's up in psychology *and* theology, he's better equipped to help them."

"Does every minister do that?" I asked.

"This one does."

M.N. opened the top drawer of her father's desk and took out pads of paper and pencils. She gave me one of each and sat down at the desk with the other. "Now," she said, "what do we know about Lisa?"

"Do you want to start with what we think might be wrong, or just the signs?"

"How much do we know about the different illnesses?" Mary Nell asked, not expecting an answer. "Not too much. We know what paranoia is, yes?"

I agreed. "And sort of what schizophrenia is."

"Right. Now, what signs of each does Lisa show?"

"You can't miss the good and bad days. There are two entirely different Lisas, day to day."

"True," M.N. said. "A classic case of split-personality."

"Then again," I remembered, "when she first showed signs of anything, she said why wouldn't people stop watching her and leave her alone. She was defensive for no reason."

"True," M.N. said again. "She imagined we were somehow criticizing her. That we were against her. A perfect example of persecution complex, otherwise known as paranoia."

"Oh, swell," I said disgustedly. "She's got two of them! Why don't we just ask your father? Maybe he could help."

"Because Daddy would simply tell us to stop muddying waters that even doctors can't clear. He'd tell us to stop playing games and to let Lisa's parents handle this. Of course, he'd be a little curious, but I think he'd forbid us to do what we want."

"So we have to do it ourselves?" I asked, worried for the first time that playing amateur Freuds could be dangerous.

"If we want to help Lisa, yes," M.N. said firmly. "Otherwise we don't *have* to *do* anything."

"So we have to do it ourselves," I said again, this time without questioning. Mary Nell is like that; if she believes strongly in something, you can't argue with her. "But still," I said unhappily, "it does sound like Lisa is twice as sick as she should be."

"We don't know that yet," M.N. said. "Tell you what. We'll start researching with the encyclopedia. That'll give us the big picture, and later we can go deeper with other books." She stood up and turned back to the bookshelves. "Here," she said, handing me an enormous volume of the *Encyclopedia Britannica*, "you take *P* for paranoia. I'll take *S* for schizophrenia. If

52

you find something that screams Lisa at you, read it aloud and we can discuss it."

I took *P* and began looking through it. M.N. got *S* and put it on the desk, taking first a minute to go into the corner to the phonograph to put on a stack of records. We had both agreed years ago that music was absolutely necessary for thinking. That night we had Dionne Warwick and Simon and Garfunkel.

I found paranoia on page 266, and then I had a sudden, worrisome thought. I flipped back to the front of the volume. "Listen," I said. "This may not be the most trustworthy sort of book. It was published in 1959. This edition, I mean."

"We have to begin somewhere, Betsy. After all, the diseases can't have changed much in such a short time."

"No, but maybe the treatments have, or the amount that's known about each illness."

"Forget it and read," M.N. said.

So I did. But I didn't get far before I interrupted again. "Listen, M.N., this isn't so hard. It says here, 'a feeling of being slighted, unappreciated, avoided and disregarded becomes a suspicion of being watched and pursued, and then slandered: plotted against, covertly attacked.' Obviously," I went on, "being slighted and unappreciated would come from just living in the same house as her parents. They couldn't care less whether Lisa lived or died."

"Betsy," M.N. said seriously, putting her own book down. "We can't accept just simple answers."

53

"But if the answers *are* simple," I argued, "there's no reason not to pay attention to them."

"But we need more than that," M.N. said positively. "We need histories and symptoms and we need to know in what direction her illness is likely to move. There are hundreds of things we need to explain."

"Explaining isn't the same thing as caring," I said softly.

"We just don't want to be conned too soon," M.N. answered. "We have a long way to go."

So I went back to my own beautiful *P*, determined to find complex answers instead of simple ones. And feeling stupid.

A few minutes later, M.N. raised her head. "You know what, Betsy? You may have been right about Lisa having two problems at the same time. Listen to this: 'The paranoid type' —of schizophrenia—'usually arising later in life than the other types, is characterized primarily by unrealistic, illogical thinking, delusions of being persecuted or of being a great person, and hallucinations.'"

"Hold on," I said. "It said that that happens later in life. Lisa's sixteen, for Pete's sake! Besides, we don't know whether she has hallucinations, do we?"

"Hang on, Sloopy, and let me finish," M.N. said, beginning to read again. "'These types of schizophrenia are by no means mutually exclusive. Mixtures are to be found, especially in the early acute phases but also in some later chronic phases.'"

"That's not a lot of help, M.N."

54

"Here's something else, though," M.N. said, for she had been reading still. " 'In addition to mixtures within schizophrenia itself, there may be mixtures of schizophrenic symptoms with those of other psychoses, notably with those of the manic-depressive group.' "

"Swell! What does *that* mean?"

"Oh, you know. Ups and downs. Good days and bad ones. Manic means up and depressive means down."

That seemed easy enough but I reached for the dictionary just the same. No luck. I stood up and got volume *M* from the shelf. I leafed through it quickly, looking for manic-depressive. Nothing.

"Ohhh, Mary Nell," I said, "this is endless! Every time they mention one thing we can understand, they mention something else we can't. We could be years learning all this stuff."

"We haven't got that much time," M.N. said. "Don't worry. We'll split the reading up between us—between us and Elizabeth, I guess, since Lisa seems to want that. Between the three of us, we'll do just fine. You'll see."

"I hope so," I said, but I was doubtful. Dionne Warwick was still trying to get to San Jose, and we were trying to find Vienna. There was a big difference.

We stopped reading then for the night because it was late and we both had homework to do for the next day. We decided that M.N. would speak to Elizabeth at lunch, and I would go back to Mr. Bernstein and ask him just to guess what might be wrong with Lisa. That would at least give us some direction in which to begin looking for answers.

As I walked home, I wondered if what we were doing was the right thing to do. After all, we would only be flailing about in a sea of books, trying to catch hold of little pieces of driftwood that came sweeping by with impossibly difficult words and ideas printed on them. They might be lifesavers in someone else's hands, but I doubted whether M.N. and I, and Elizabeth, were strong enough to throw them out to Lisa. The distance between us was growing greater every day.

★ **10** ★

The next day, instead of waiting until lunch to get to Mr. Bernstein, I went to school early to tell him what we were doing to help Lisa. He listened, swiveling back and forth gently in his chair. He seemed to think what we were doing was futile. He did tell me where to go if I were really interested in learning about mental illnesses, and he offered to lend me some of his books if I promised to take care of them and return them to his office each day. I saw myself trudging to and from school every day with forty pounds of words and no pictures. I thanked him anyway.

In spite of the incident beneath Mr. Milne's desk, Mr. Bernstein still needed to be convinced before he risked anything. Even then, later, when and if he did help, he would probably do it through other people.

From some people you learn to expect nothing fast. Mr. Bernstein wasn't one of these, exactly, but he had his own hang-ups about getting deeply involved in anything. So when he said he might be able to talk to me occasionally about Lisa and perhaps help direct our sessions through me, I was grateful he had come that far out of his particular shadow, even if he wanted only to stick one toe in the spotlight.

Having got to Bernstein early, I was able to join M.N. at lunch when she talked to Elizabeth. I found them at a table in the cafeteria during first lunch. Mary Nell's plate, as usual, was full of fattening things. She puts mayonnaise on everything and it never seems to make any difference to her figure. Elizabeth sat quietly, listening, with a fruit salad and some diet crackers in front of her.

"How far have you got?" I asked as I sat down.

"We're just beginning," M.N. said, trying to catch a glob of mayonnaise as it slid out of a sandwich into the air. She missed. "I've just told Elizabeth what we think about Lisa. I mean, that she needs help and isn't going to get it anywhere except from us."

"What do you think?" I asked Elizabeth.

57

"I think you're probably right," she said expressionlessly. "So what?"

"So," M.N. said, "*we* have to help her."

"How?" asked Elizabeth.

M.N. paused for a second. "How?" Elizabeth asked again.

"You're no easier about this than Lisa is," M.N. said curtly.

"I'll tell you something, Mary Nell," Elizabeth answered. "You're right about Lisa. You can't even begin to imagine how sick she is. But if you're going to sign up here, you have to expect a lot of rough play."

Elizabeth's tone wasn't patronizing, exactly. Just impressive. M.N. sat still for a minute, looking at Elizabeth without blinking.

"Elizabeth," I said. "Lisa said something last night about you, about how maybe you could help. Will you?"

Elizabeth smiled, more to herself than to me. It was a little chilling. "You still haven't answered my question," she said. "How do you expect to help her?"

"Well," said M.N. between bites (she had recovered), "we told her we know. That *we* believe she's ill even if her parents don't. That we want to do whatever we can for her."

"Which is?" Elizabeth wanted to know.

"We are going to ... well, therapy-ize her," M.N. answered, a little embarrassed.

"How?" Elizabeth asked for what seemed the tenth time.

"By talking with her," I said. "By letting her know we care. She can talk about it, I think.

58

She did a little last night. We would be a kind of decompression chamber for her. A place where she'll know people understand, and—"

"You can't," Elizabeth said flatly.

"Can't what?" M.N. asked.

"Understand," Elizabeth replied. "You can't."

"Well," M.N. said, "we *might* be able to. After all, we do care, and we're the only ones who do."

"So what?" Elizabeth said. "Caring and being able to understand are not the same thing."

"Now *you* listen to *me!*" M.N. said, having had it by this time. "You can criticize if you want, tell us we're idiots. The only question that matters is, will you help us anyway?"

Elizabeth Frazer smiled again, this time directly at us. "Yes," she said after a minute. "All right."

Mary Nell's shoulders sank a little in relief, and she was able to begin eating again. *At last!* I could tell she was thinking. Mary Nell is very fond of food.

"Elizabeth," I said, "may I ask a question, a sort of personal one?"

Elizabeth looked quickly at me and picked up her tray. "No, Betsy," she said, standing up. "You may not."

She walked away to leave her tray on a clearing table on the way out of the cafeteria. I watched her go, a tall, blonde girl who seemed contained from within by taut wires strung from shoulder to shoulder, from head to hip.

59

Self-contained and beautiful and distant, and suddenly mysterious. I was mostly concerned for Lisa, of course, but I knew now we had another stone to overturn.

★ 11 ★

At the end of school that day, we all met on the front steps to wait for Lisa. Elizabeth stood next to M.N., watching kids pour out of classes, jump into cars or walk in groups to the nearby shopping center to hang around doing nothing. M.N. faced another direction, hawk-eyed for Lisa. I watched the side of the building, in case Lisa should come out a side door and miss us.

Which is exactly what she did. Miss us, I mean. She never appeared from any direction at all. M.N. went back into the building while Elizabeth and I circled it, in opposite directions, just in case.

We didn't find her. Elizabeth and I thought Lisa had probably just forgotten about meeting us after class. M.N. was convinced she had escaped on purpose, that Lisa had a sly streak a mile long and that this was just the beginning of deceptions and broken promises. (It seemed to me that M.N. had stayed up rather later than I the night before, reading more than encyclopedias.)

The thing was, though, you had to sympathize with Lisa. None of us was certain what exactly we were going to do for her that afternoon.

So our good intent for the day was ignored. We had no idea where Lisa was or what she was doing. "Don't worry about it," Elizabeth told us. "If Lisa really believes you care and want to help, she'll come when she feels she needs you. So long," she said, walking off by herself.

On our way home, M.N. was furious. "I don't know where Elizabeth Frazer gets her nerve! I really don't. It was *our* idea to help Lisa, not hers. All we asked was her help. She could have refused if she thought we were doing something stupid."

"She's not doing anything for *us*," I said. "It has only to do with Lisa."

"Still and all," Mary Nell said, "her attitude could be better. *We're* trying to help Lisa, too."

"I guess Elizabeth has something we don't," I said. "It certainly grabbed Lisa. We can't afford to lose her now because she seems sort of cold. *We* don't need her. Lisa does. So," I said smiling, "smile."

"Nuts!" Mary Nell said, turning off to her street. "The whole thing just reeks!"

I got home and decided to get my sister's old psychology books out of the basement. She kept all her books from college hoping that maybe, someday, she could go back and graduate. After, of course, she'd had a couple of kids and got them in school so she'd have the time. But I could find only one, which must have been the basic book in her beginning course.

It was a sort of survey, looking at lots of different things very fast. Mostly, as far as I could tell, it was about behavior. The way the authors went about studying this was through rats. Not very helpful, but I dug in anyway.

In an hour, I had learned about rats and mazes, Pavlov's theory (all those poor dogs!), and the approach-avoidance conflict. I hung onto this last, because it seemed about the only useful information in the whole book. What it is is when someone wants to do something and yet knows he shouldn't, he reaches out for the thing he shouldn't have, remembers he shouldn't have it, and pulls back. He can go through this for hours, days, years, which makes him absolutely motionless, afraid to do anything. It's the sort of thing that could really hang you up.

After a while, though, I'd had it with rats and one poor guy who was so confused he couldn't move. I wanted stronger stuff—you know, case histories of really grim people. But there weren't any in this book so I put it aside and settled for the late afternoon movie.

In case you haven't noticed, I know a lot about movies. Not trivia, like who lifted Joan Crawford up in the third number of *Our Dancing Daughters*, but about individual movies, what happened and who the stars were, and what they did afterward and so forth. I like

Tuesday Weld a lot, and Steve McQueen, and a few others, but these really don't compare with great actors like John Mills, Geraldine Page, or Cliff Robertson. About the only *new* person I'm hooked on is Cher. She must be the funniest, and sometimes the sexiest, lady going. Of course, I'm partial to Paul Newman. I hate to say it, but it *is* his eyes. I also have a feeling, though, that he's a *nice* guy, too, which makes it O.K. for me to join the mob. I mean I like his eyes, but for me there's more to him than that—like his body. Zowee!!!

Anyway, I turned on the television set in our game room and waited for it to warm up. At last (we have a very old television set) the picture came on. It was *Raintree County*.

I'd seen this about a thousand times, but suddenly I had a new idea. I grabbed the phone and dialed like crazy.

"M.N.?" I said. "Listen, they've got *Raintree County* on the Early Show. Yeah. So listen, you remember Liz Taylor goes bats, right? Maybe if we watch it hard, we'll see something of Lisa in it. What? Well, then, I will, anyway. I'll call you later if anything comes up, O.K.? O.K. Bye."

Elizabeth Taylor, in case you haven't seen this thing, is gorgeous—as an actress, I mean. For the first time (except for maybe *A Place in the Sun*) she really got her teeth into something and did a fair job of being someone else besides Elizabeth Taylor. She plays this lost sort of Southern belle who goes slowly nuts (it's a very long movie) and finally dies, leaving

63

Montgomery Clift free to marry Eva Marie Saint who has been so patient you can't stand it for years and years and years. (I mean, it's a *very* long movie!)

Anyway, comparisons were obvious. So I settled in. After all, I thought, even though it's a movie, people take a lot of care to make things real and lifelike. The real-er something is, mostly the better it is. And Taylor had gotten an Academy Award nomination for it, so she must have caught the real thing in part, anyway. She must have studied some psychology to get the reality of her role and to play a madwoman convincingly.

That's what I thought. Actually, I love the movie. So I sank into the corner of the couch, pulled up my legs, and put on my glasses. I was in heaven.

After about forty minutes, the doorbell rang. I didn't move, because my brother was around somewhere. A couple of minutes later, he was standing in the doorway.

"One of your screwy friends is here," he said.

I looked up. "Who?"

"Lisa Shilling," he said, twirling his finger around his ear. I could have killed him.

I jumped up, switched off the set and got into my shoes in one motion, and ran to the front door. There she was. Just standing, waiting. "Come in," I said, and smiled.

"Thanks, Betsy," she said, following me back into the game room.

We sat down. Neither one of us said anything. I just didn't know what to say.

64

"I couldn't find Elizabeth," Lisa said at last. "I guess she didn't go straight home."

"She was waiting for you out front," I told her.

"Oh," Lisa said.

"Yeah," I said. It wasn't the most satisfactory conversation ever held. "Listen, would you like a drink or something? We've got one of everything."

"Do I make you nervous?" Lisa asked.

I stopped. "Yes," I said. "A little."

"I'm glad you said that. Promise me something."

"What?"

"That you'll always be honest."

"Oh," I said. "I am most of the time, really."

"But with me," Lisa said, "you must *always* be."

"O.K. That's not so hard."

"Mary Nell won't be, you know," Lisa told me.

"Why on earth not? She's about the most direct person I ever met."

"Yes, but she won't be with me. She wants to shield me," Lisa said. "She wants to be kind. People who want to be kind without understanding are almost always dishonest."

"But that's unfair," I objected. "Really, Lisa, she'll do the best she can. I know she will."

Lisa smiled a little. "I know. I know she will. But her best won't be as good as yours."

Well! What do you say to something like that? "Shall I get Elizabeth on the phone?" I asked.

65

"If you like," Lisa said, getting up to turn the television set on. I waited a minute, until she was comfortable, and then I went into the kitchen to phone Elizabeth—and Mary Nell.

Three minutes later, when I came back, Lisa had disappeared.

I looked around and then ran to find my brother. He hadn't seen or heard anything.

I shrugged, deciding there wasn't much I could do, and went back into the game room. *Raintree County* was still on, and I had just gotten comfortable again when the doorbell rang a second time. This time I ran to get it right away. It was Elizabeth. I had forgotten she was coming.

"Hi," I said.

"Hello," she said, coming in. "Where's Lisa?"

"I haven't the foggiest."

"What do you mean? I thought she was here when you phoned."

"She was. And when I phoned M.N., too. But when I went back into the game room, she was gone."

"Oh, well," Elizabeth said turning around, get-

66

ting ready to leave, "I guess we have to expect things like this."

"Why don't you stay a while," I offered. "M.N. will be here in a second, so we may as well do something."

Elizabeth looked at me a minute and then she smiled a little. "All right," she said. I motioned her into the room where the set was still going, and then M.N. rang the bell.

I told her, as we walked to the back of the house, about Lisa's disappearance.

"There are two reasons that's ridiculous," M.N. said. "Oh, hi," she said to Elizabeth.

"Which two?" Elizabeth asked.

"Well, first, to come and ask for help, as best she can, I mean, and then run off. Second, why come to Betsy? She knows this was all my idea, and she has some kind of confidence in you. Why come to Betsy at all?"

It was a thought that hadn't occurred to me. *Why not?* I thought now, but I agreed it was strange.

"I can tell you," Elizabeth said. "She has less to fear from Betsy than from us."

"Less to fear!" M.N. nearly shouted. "I'm reading my eyes out trying to find answers, trying to—"

"That's just it, M.N.," Elizabeth broke in. "It isn't going to help doing that, trying to find answers. There aren't any you can find in books."

"Now look, Elizabeth Frazer," M.N. said. "I don't understand a lot of what's going on here, but I can tell you one thing. What we have here is either a paranoid or a schizophrenic, and maybe both together. The only way we can even begin to help is by understanding the symptoms and labeling them, so we know exactly what we're working with."

"Mary Nell," Elizabeth said pleasantly. "May I suggest something?"

M.N. waited. So did I.

"You can't expect to label this," Elizabeth said. "The only thing we know we have is a psychotic personality. How psychotic or serious we can't know. Mental illness is something you play by ear, believe me. You can't treat it as a math problem that has a logical solution. You won't do Lisa any good if you go at it that way."

Something in the way Elizabeth said this brought M.N. up short. She sighed. "But anyway," she said, "why come to Betsy?"

"As I said," Elizabeth explained, "Lisa feels more secure with her than with you. Maybe she knows you want to label and dissect and perform the operation. Betsy, in her own way, wants to help as badly, but she doesn't judge. She *feels* for Lisa, instead." I blushed. "No, Betsy," Elizabeth said, "don't. You have something neither M.N. nor I have, and it's a very, very good thing to have, so hang onto it."

"What is it, for heaven's sake?" I asked.

"Warmth. A naturalness. A simplicity. It's about the best therapy Lisa could ever have."

Well! Of all the things I hadn't ever wanted to be it was natural, warm, and simple. I've been working for years to become hard, sophisticated, worldly, and exciting. All that effort, all that time—all shot to hell! I smiled.

Elizabeth smiled back. "It could be worse," she said.

"I guess," I answered, shrugging.

"But *I'm* her friend!" M.N. shouted. "I want to help her!"

"You will," Elizabeth said as nicely as she could. "You will, but you have to relax about it. The thing is that—"

There was a knock on a door. Elizabeth stopped talking and looked at me. The sound came again. I looked around.

Our game room is simple, and it looks like this: nothing fancy, but there is one wall of glass that opens onto the back yard where there's a patio and a grill for cooking out. Another wall is all bookshelves, lots of *Reader's Digest Condensed Books* and magazines and the books the three of us had as kids. The third wall has an archway that leads into the hall going toward the front of the house. And the fourth wall has a fireplace with a few pictures above it and, on the right, a closet in which there is stereo stuff and records and a bar.

I jumped up and ran to the closet door, putting my ear to the wood and waiting. The knock came again, and it *was* from inside. I opened the door and there was Lisa, sitting on the floor, looking up at me.

I turned to face Elizabeth and M.N. Lisa stood up and came out of the closet. "Hi," she said to everyone and to no one in particular.

She walked into the room and sat down on the floor, in the middle of things.

"Anyone want anything to drink?" I offered. It was a stupid thing to say, but I said it anyway.

"I'll have something," Elizabeth said to help me. "But it has to be a diet thing."

"Me, too," M.N. said.

"Nothing for me, thanks," Lisa said from the floor.

I turned back into the closet to the small ice-box and glasses and stuff. No one said anything while I poured and handed the drinks around.

"Do you think we could turn the T.V. off?" Lisa asked. "It makes me a little nervous."

"Sure," I said, and I did.

"Why does that make you nervous?" M.N. asked.

"I guess it hits a little close to home," Lisa said.

"What does? Her sickness?" Elizabeth asked.

"No. Not that, really. It's the scene in the ... in the insane asylum, when he finally tracks her down."

"But, Lisa," I said, "that was a hundred years ago. Things can't be that bad now."

"I haven't the faintest idea. Yet," she said.

"I read something the other day," M.N. said, "about just that sort of thing. About how while there are still a few of those older places, dungeons really, there are lots of new places, sort of communities, where life goes on normally, and everyone—"

70

"I read it, too, M.N.," Lisa said. "Forget it."

There was a pause.

"Well," Lisa said, her voice changing a little, "let's not all sit here staring. Amuse yourselves. Ask questions. Poke about a bit. Maybe we'll all find it together."

"Bull!" said Elizabeth. It was a shocker, coming from her.

"What do you mean?" Lisa asked angrily.

"I mean bull!" Elizabeth answered. "If you want to play at sympathy and roses, you can hire people for that."

Lisa looked at Elizabeth for a very long minute. Then she smiled. "Right," she said.

No one said anything then, for a time. You could hear breathing, and the tinkle of ice in glasses, and the rustle of a skirt against a chair-cover as someone shifted.

"What terrifies me," Lisa said in an odd, small voice, "is that I don't know when it's coming, or what to expect. I try to keep track of things, but then everything gets away from me anyway. Later, when I've got the upper hand again, I'm not sure whether I was dreaming or whether something actually happened."

"Like what?" I asked.

"What does go on?" M.N. wanted to know.

"All kinds of crazy things," Lisa said, smiling a little. "I mean, I make dates with people who don't exist. I hear people who aren't there. Just shadows, who talk to me and seem to make sense most of the time. They have beautiful voices, English, I guess, and I love to listen to them. It's like one long dream, really. I hear

71

everything and I do everything, and I also see everything. I watch things happen. I watch me, too, right in the middle of it. It's like a movie, only better. I'm the star. It makes me wake up at night giggling, and sometimes it puts me to sleep in broad daylight. I can do that now, you know—sleep with my eyes open. It's heaven."

"Zowee!" I said. "Next time you fall asleep in class or something, nudge me. I'd love to see how you do it. You could make a fortune teaching us all."

"I know. That was one of the first things I thought of," Lisa said laughing.

But her laughter changed. It became deeper, and then it was like a sudden violent series of coughs, a hacking sound. We waited and when it was over, Lisa looked around at us. "Come on," she said. "What are you waiting for? Why give a damn now? Why am I worth more now?"

It was her English voice again, deep and strong and husky, clipped and terrifying. "One is, after all, the same bloody person! What do you want from me now?"

"Lisa," Elizabeth said.

"I'm quite sick of it all! Sick to death! Of you all, too," Lisa went on, looking squarely at M.N. Mary Nell blanched. "Yes, yes, I am. You, too!"

"But Lisa," Mary Nell began.

"Don't give me any of that," Lisa said quickly. "You're always so damned smart, planning and organizing everything. This is all *your* good work, this whole thing!"

I thought M.N. was going to burst into

72

tears, but Elizabeth reached over and touched her arm.

"You are quite the most rotten, sneaky, conniving little person I've ever known," Lisa went on, really rolling now. It was amazing. "You are, yes. You've always wanted Brian for yourself. You and everyone else I know. You've always envied me. Hated me. That's why you planned everything, so very carefully planned it all. You and Brian and all of you! Getting the teachers in it, though, that was the clever thing. Oh yes, that was cleverer than clever, even more than paying my parents off."

"Lisa!" Elizabeth shouted, standing up. "Lisa! Stop it!"

Lisa looked up at Elizabeth with something close to hatred in her eyes. They held each other's glance for the longest minute I'd ever lived through, and then something seemed to break. Lisa slumped and began to cry, silently at first but then loudly a moment later. It was a rasping sound, still in a strange tone, and it began to change as we all were still, shocked. It, her voice I mean, as she was crying, moved back up the scale somehow and in a minute she was Lisa again, crying as Lisa would, I guess, if she were the real Lisa.

By that time, M.N. *was* crying, sort of shaking and just letting tears streak down her cheeks. She sat on the couch, her arms at her sides, crying right along with Lisa.

Finally Lisa slowed down a little. As she did, she looked up at Mary Nell, who hadn't slowed down at all. Abruptly, Lisa's tears stopped and

her look was one of concern and love, and then
shame. She stood up and went to M.N.

For a second Lisa simply stood next to M.N.
Then she touched her shoulder very gently.
"Help me," she whispered.

Then she turned, walked out of the game
room and out of the house altogether, ex-
hausted.

★ **13** ★

M.N. bounced back.

Elizabeth reminded us both that if we were
going to try to help Lisa, we had to expect
almost anything. It was good to care about
Lisa, and to love her in a way, but there would
be times when we couldn't allow ourselves to be
hurt or upset by her.

So M.N. got all fired up again. She dug out
her library card and began to devour book after
book, calling me up at all hours to read bits
about schizophrenia or about paranoia—getting
excited by each new piece of information and
each new discovery.

It was marvelous therapy. For M.N. Pretty
soon, though, both Elizabeth and I could see
where it was leading. M.N. began diagnosing

everyone. No one escaped. No one was free of neuroses or symptoms, latent or overt. She was having a field day.

Among others, she analyzed Mr. Bernstein, Mr. Milne, Miss Strane our calculus teacher (that was a marvel!), her own father, my father, and both of Lisa's parents. It was about then that I remembered the saying, "A little knowledge is a dangerous thing." Whoever said that first must have known M.N. was on the way.

But when we talked to Lisa, it was M.N. who talked least. I could see why. Though she had pretty well recovered, M.N. was still wary of Lisa.

Not Elizabeth, though. Elizabeth seldom spoke but when she did it somehow mattered more than when M.N. or I did. She seemed to be a step ahead of Lisa. It was she who could calm Lisa if she needed it, or guide her thoughts in a meaningful way. I was fascinated by everything she did, but Elizabeth and I never really got any closer as friends.

Oddly, M.N. and I did. One of the changes that took place after that one afternoon's disaster was M.N.'s renewed spirit, as I said. But she had lost confidence, too. Lisa was a shock for M.N. who had always been the brightest, the most hard-working, the best-liked girl around. She loved to organize, to arrange, to be chairman. And she was good at all these things.

All of a sudden, M.N. wasn't in charge of *anything*, and she wanted to talk about it. She needed a confidante. And as M.N.'s confidence sank, mine miraculously rose to the surface. I could have sworn I actually felt myself growing up, maturing. Naturally, just when I was beginning to feel that maybe I did know a little about life, M.N. jumped ship and swam to her father.

I gather M.N. decided if she could involve her father in what we were doing, she would be reinstated as chief, leader, executive-in-charge. It hadn't yet occurred to her that Lisa, one individual human being, simply wasn't going to be taken over or solved or maneuvered to M.N.'s satisfaction.

So M.N. talked to her father, and he told her what she told me long ago he would say: that it was a dangerous thing to do. That we were playing in a swimming pool in midwinter that could be drained at any minute, leaving us all open to pneumonia, and probably drowning Lisa at the same time. But, and this must have been what M.N. counted on, while Mr. Fickett thought we shouldn't have been involved, he thought he might be able to do something we couldn't if *he* were involved.

So Mr. Fickett got hold of Mr. Milne, our English teacher. He decided that what had to be said would count more coming from real-er, more serious and responsible people than from dopey teen-agers. When M.N. told me this I got a little hot, but I remembered that it wasn't who did the trick that counted, it was whether the trick was done at all that could help Lisa.

The problem was that while Mr. Fickett wanted to help Lisa, all he and Mr. Milne really knew was what they had either heard from M.N., or what Mr. Milne had seen in school in only one of Lisa's classes. It wasn't a lot of ammunition.

Still, all the Shillings could do was say no, they didn't agree and weren't about to admit their daughter was going nuts; or yes, they did see the danger and would spare nothing to help her. It was a 50-50 chance of getting through.

So Mr. Fickett made an appointment pretending, I guess, that it had something to do with the church. It sounded a little dishonest for a minister to get his foot in the door that way, but I figured Mr. Fickett was old enough to handle his own conscience. The cause was what was important.

When Mr. Fickett and Mr. Milne arrived at the Shillings', Mrs. Shilling had gone out, no doubt busily pretending to be some sort of society lady, which she badly wanted to be, fooling no one but herself. (I may have mentioned that she's not my favorite lady of all time.) This left just the three men, M.N. said, which suited everyone fine.

"Mr. Shilling," M.N.'s father began, "we have a problem."

"Which I gather," Mr. Shilling said, "has nothing to do with your church. Unless Mr. Milne here is a deacon or something."

"Not me," Mr. Milne said smiling. "I'm one of those sandwich board carriers you see, whose church comes in the form of believing in man."

"Which, in theory, is the best kind of reli-

77

gion," Mr. Fickett said. "No, the problem is your daughter, Lisa."

"Is she in trouble?" Mr. Shilling asked. "Has she broken into the church? Looted her classroom?"

"Of course not," Mary Nell's father said. "You know your daughter better than that."

"That's very true," Mr. Shilling agreed quickly.

"What you may be unaware of, though," Mr. Fickett went on, "is that Lisa is in more serious trouble, a kind that calls for special handling."

Mr. Shilling laughed harshly. "Gentlemen," he said, "you're not going to tell me she's pregnant!"

"Not," Mr. Milne said, "as far as we know. If she were, I can't think it would be so amusing as you do."

"She's ill, Mr. Shilling, mentally," Mr. Fickett said.

Mr. Shilling stopped chuckling. "Do I understand you, Reverend? Are you about to tell me Lisa is losing her mind?"

"It seems to us that that, in theory, is the present danger," Mr. Fickett replied.

"Your daughter said the same thing to my wife not long ago," Mr. Shilling said, "no doubt at *my* daughter's urging. At the time, as I recall, neither my wife nor I was much impressed by their logic."

"You should have been," Mr. Milne said. "It might have made a difference in terms of time."

"A while back, an imaginative child came to tell my wife that Lisa was going crazy. I'm not

78

unreasonable, and I'm not a villain. But what's the evidence? What do you see we can't?"

"Well, *I* see her every day in school," Mr. Milne answered. "I can honestly say her behavior is anything but strictly rational."

"Does it vary so much from your own?" Mr. Shilling asked.

"Well, I admit I'm not overconsistent," Mr. Milne said, smiling politely. "But I don't think I appear to have separate personalities. I don't have the ups and downs your daughter has. I don't hide from the world half the time and then shout to be recognized by it the other half. And, I'm afraid, when I make a mistake, I don't imagine an entire class has laid a deliberate trap for me. I accept the results of my own behavior."

"Mr. Shilling," M.N.'s father said, "your daughter has admitted to her friends that she thinks she's ill. That she is frightened. In theory, you are the person who can best help her."

"I agree," Mr. Shilling said. "I really do. And I'd be the first to help if I thought Lisa were really experiencing a trauma of some terrible kind."

"You don't think she is?" Mr. Milne asked.

"I haven't the faintest idea whether she is or not," Mr. Shilling said. "All I can tell you positively is that we—my wife and I—don't see signs of anything disturbing. Lisa's behavior is as normal as it's ever been."

"But what about the reports from her school?" Mr. Fickett asked. "Don't they disturb you at all? Isn't there a chance that we might be right? After all, you sent her away for *some* reason."

"Yes, we did," Mr. Shilling admitted. "We were told to, and we could, so we did. Since then, there haven't been any other incidents like that first one. We see nothing different. Gentlemen, I'm a very busy man. I travel a great deal. When I am here, I can't tell if anything abnormal is happening or has happened unless I'm told about it. No one has said anything further. Lisa has done nothing more. She goes about life as she chooses. She does what she feels is right and in tune with our way of living."

"I think she's marching to another tune now," Mr. Milne offered. "I agree with you. If you can't see it, perhaps it isn't there. But that's mental illness. It can't be seen. Be grateful sometimes it can be sensed."

"I appreciate your concern, Mr. Milne," said Lisa's father. "But my nose just isn't as keen as yours. Lisa's never been a timid child. When she wanted something, she always said so. She wants something now—God knows what!—and she's saying so."

"That's unjust," said Mr. Milne.

"Perhaps," Mr. Shilling said. "Maybe it's not that simple."

"The simple fact is," Mary Nell's father said suddenly, "that if you don't help your daughter, someone else will. We owe it to her."

Mr. Shilling spoke very quietly and very slowly. "Mr. Fickett," he said, "this is not a film. If I don't help Lisa, you can't. I'm not irrational or unfeeling. Don't start imagining you can claim either her mother or me is unfit as a parent. We've given Lisa everything she could want. She's been free to live her own way, choose her own friends, form her own ideas. She's well-fed, decently clothed, publicly educated. There's nothing wrong with Lisa's upbringing any more than there is anything wrong with those who brought her up, or with you and your family."

No one spoke for a minute. I guess Mary Nell's father was trying to think of something really devastating to say, and Mr. Milne was waiting to find out what it was going to be. But they waited too long.

"Goddamn you!" Lisa screamed, twisting around a door and nearly leaping into the room. "Go on! Go on! Don't stop now! Think of something, do something, do anything!"

"Lisa!" called her father furiously.

"No!" she shouted back. "I want help! I need help! I need it! Do something for God's sake! No, do it for *my* sake!"

She turned, already running, and disappeared.

Elizabeth spoke first. "The trouble with reasonable adult human beings is that they collapse when they meet other reasonable adult human beings. We don't."

We had decided immediately, when we knew that Mr. Fickett and Mr. Milne hadn't found that devastating argument we all needed, what to do next. The vague idea we had had about group therapy simply had to be put into action. We had to get Lisa to open up, to lean on us and depend on us and to share her illness with us so that it wouldn't seem so frightening, so lonely.

Mr. Fickett had come to us earlier to say that he thought the best thing we could do was not get involved any further in Lisa's problems. That perhaps her parents would come around by themselves and realize what she needed.

I think Mr. Fickett was beginning to worry that all this might be having an "unhealthy" effect on the three of us. But he was worrying about the wrong thing. He knew he was right to be concerned, but he didn't want to be concerned about the right thing.

"At least they tried," M.N. said. "Maybe Mr. Shilling just needs time to think."

"He wants the time *not* to think," Elizabeth said quickly. "He'd like to forget the whole thing."

"I would too," I said, "if I were in his place. It can't be any fun having people tell you your kid's going nuts."

"But you wouldn't ignore that," Elizabeth said.

The doorbell rang then, and M.N. went to let Lisa in.

Before this, though, M.N. had formed a plan. She had a legal-size pad of paper and a pencil on her father's desk to take notes on. Elizabeth and I were supposed to be as natural as possible and get Lisa to free-associate. This was one of M.N.'s new terms, which meant to start talking about one thing and then float on to another, and then on again to something else, finally sitting there blabbing about whatever came into your head. M.N. had read somewhere that when someone did this, he dropped "clues" as he went along that any half-witted listener could decipher and understand.

M.N. had decided to be the half-wit.

"Hi," Lisa said as she came into the room ahead of M.N.

"Hi," I said, wondering instantly if that meant something special to M.N. now.

"Well," Lisa said, sinking down onto the

83

floor in her usual wrapped-up position, "we didn't win the game, did we?"

"Not yet," Elizabeth said.

"I scared the hell out of Daddy, though," Lisa said happily. "I don't remember trying to do just that, but that's certainly what I did. He's *still* drinking."

"At least someone else tried to help for a change," said M.N.

"I wonder if trying is the whole thing," Lisa answered. "Not really, though. I mean, I don't really wonder. It's just something you say."

Mary Nell scratched something on her pad. Loudly. I winced.

"How do you feel?" Elizabeth asked Lisa.

"Tired. Always tired," Lisa said. "What it is is that I never get any rest. I mean, when I'm asleep, I'm not."

"What do you mean?" I asked.

"Well, my mind doesn't stop any more," Lisa said. "It's more than just having a lot of dreams, one after another."

"Do you have a lot of dreams?" M.N. asked, pencil poised.

"No," Lisa said, thinking a moment. I could see M.N. was disappointed. "It's like being in a lecture course. I'm being talked at all the time."

"Can't you tune out once in a while?" Elizabeth asked. "I mean if you're listening to a lecture, your mind wanders around anyway the minute the thing gets dull."

"Not with me," Lisa said. "I'm made to listen. It's as though I have to understand every-

84

thing very fast because there's going to be a quiz when it's over. So I listen, straining to catch every funny sounding word and trying to put all the meanings together so that if I'm called on I won't fail."

"Who's your teacher?" M.N. asked, raising her head from her busy scribbling.

"No one person in particular. Lots of people. English people," Lisa answered.

"Umm," M.N. said, nodding. "I see. Go on."

But Lisa started to laugh instead. And so did I. I think we had both caught a picture of M.N. with a beard and pince-nez, nodding sagely.

"Shall I lie on the couch, M.N.?" Lisa finally asked. "Wouldn't that be better?"

"Yes, it probably would help," M.N. said seriously. "Just make yourself comfortable and keep talking. Say anything that comes into your head."

Lisa got up and went to the couch and stretched out on it. There was a funny glint in her eye. Elizabeth looked at me and winked, motioning toward M.N. Lisa assumed a thoughtful pose.

"Well," she began, "I do have funny dreams once in a while."

"Oh!" M.N. said, turning to a new page of her notebook.

"Yes," Lisa went on. "Mostly in color and wide-screen, with fantastically good soundtracks."

"You feel you're in a theater, watching a movie?" M.N. asked.

85

"That's it exactly!" Lisa cried, a little too quickly. But she caught herself.

"Tell us about your dreams," said Elizabeth in a very deep, very phony tone. Mary Nell was writing frantically.

"Well," Lisa said slowly, "usually they all start the same way."

"Yes?" M.N. said, writing madly.

"Yes. There's a kind of fog on the screen, swirling around and around, changing colors all the time. And just when I think it's beginning to clear—"

"Yes, yes," M.N. muttered.

"It gets thick all over again," Lisa said.

"Um-hmm."

"Very interesting," Elizabeth growled low. "Very interesting."

"Then, of course, there's music, too," Lisa continued.

"What kind of music?" Mary Nell asked.

"Mostly rock," Lisa answered. "Lots of times it's *Mrs. Robinson*."

"Really?" M.N. said happily. "Really? That's incredible."

"I know," Lisa said. "Anyway, finally the fog begins to clear, and I can see very tall, very straight pine trees. Just the tops of them."

I checked. Mary Nell was in ecstasy: head down, lower lip pulled in, a happy scowl on her forehead, and all the time her hand flew across and back on the pad, pencil bobbing up and down measuring her excitement. Poor M.N.

"The trees seem to come from nowhere, just a kind of greenish-bluish fog, and the music

86

goes on and gets sort of weird, sort of Ravi Shankarish. You know?" Lisa said.

"Go on, go on," M.N. answered. "Don't stop."

"Well, finally the fog clears, and you can see that the trees grow in a desert."

"A desert," M.N. repeated.

"Yes. It's brown and dry and very hot, but there's no sun at all," Lisa said.

"No sun," M.N. chorused.

"And then I see it. Crawling through the sand."

"What? What is it?" M.N.'s head came up fast.

"It's a ... it's a ..." Lisa played it out. "Well, it's a sort of snake."

Mary Nell stared at Lisa, and then got purple.

"A snake," Lisa said again. "And then suddenly there are lots of snakes, all around, all crawling toward the same thing."

Elizabeth started to giggle and so did I. Mary Nell was horrified. I guess she couldn't yet see where Lisa was leading her, and Lisa has had a tendency since she's been ill to be a little raunchy at times.

"They're crawling through the sand, going around microphones—"

"Microphones!" M.N. gasped.

"Slithering through a sea of waving fingers—"

"Oh, no!"

"Moving toward a huge, enormous, gigantic—"

"Don't!" Mary Nell screamed. "Don't say it!"

87

"Hole!" Lisa shouted and doubled up hysterically.

M.N. looked as though she'd been to war. Elizabeth and I couldn't hold back any longer and we howled. We laughed and giggled and rolled on the floor, pointing at M.N. and hooting, calling her "Freud" and "doctor" and "genius."

M.N. just stared at us all, probably wondering if what Lisa had had all this time had suddenly become contagious.

Finally she nodded. "O.K., you guys," she said. "O.K."

It took us another two or three minutes to get ourselves under control again, as M.N. tore off the pages she'd written and put them in a drawer, carefully folded, no doubt for later reading.

"And then," Lisa said, no longer smiling, "and then, there is my father. Or rather, there isn't my father."

No one moved. No one even breathed.

"But that's for some other time," Lisa said, getting up off the couch. "That's for some other day," she said and walked out of M.N.'s house on her heels.

☆ 15 ☆

"I decided you shouldn't be doing this alone," Mr. Bernstein said, "so I called her teachers together and we discussed what realistically we could do."

"Was Mr. Jackson there, too?" I asked.

"No," Mr. Bernstein said. "The principal's a very busy man. He might misunderstand what we were saying and dismiss Miss Shilling altogether, as though by getting rid of her somehow helped her, too. It wouldn't, of course."

I nodded. Mr. Bernstein seemed to be fighting for time, and I realized that whatever he and Lisa's teachers had decided to do probably wouldn't be enough.

"The difficulty is, Miss Goodman, that we have two responsibilities. To Lisa, and to the others, her classmates. How can we help her without hurting the others? And, too, there are the parents. You know how much trouble parents can cause when they want to."

I remembered the school strike in New York City, with parents trying to run schools, and teachers disagreeing, and no schools being run at all. Out where we live it probably wouldn't have been so bad, but we've had times too when parents, just one set, caused enough trouble for a whole town.

Then something else hit me. Bernstein and the teachers were being more than cautious. They were afraid of Lisa's parents. Plain and simple afraid. I sighed and tried very hard to remember that teachers are human, too, and must have problems that sometimes make them do things they don't want to.

"You are reading my mind, perhaps?" Mr. Bernstein asked me.

"What you mean is that there isn't anything you can do that won't make the Shillings furious, or put yourselves and Mr. Jackson in a bad position."

"Not quite," he said. "Some of her teachers realize what is wrong. Especially one of them, your Mr. Milne."

"What about the others?"

"We *all* agree on one thing. Final exams are not far away. For the sake of the other students, we decided that Lisa should be left alone, under your care. We may be able to help by keeping her with us and exercising whatever control we can. After all, it's better for her to be here in school with us than on the loose somewhere. But one of you must always be at her side. The teachers will help if you need it and if they can. She will not be asked questions unless she volunteers. She will not be disturbed by anyone. And then, when it is all over, the responsibility will be her family's, as it should be."

It wasn't much, I thought to myself. In fact, it wasn't anything. But I decided to be bright about it. We had made our point with Lisa's teachers and they finally agreed something was wrong. At least we didn't have to worry about Lisa in class any more, unless she got a bee in her bonnet. I pictured Lisa spending each day with her hands tied at her sides and her mouth taped shut.

"Well," I said to Mr. Bernstein, "it's not much, but it does simplify things. Thank you."

"It's small, but it might help," he said.

I nodded. And then I gave him my Joanne Woodward smile—the one that starts slow along one side of my face and then spreads—to say "thank you" again. For whatever *his* problems were, Mr. Bernstein had done something. He had allowed himself to be drawn in a little.

On my way to the cafeteria, I flipped back in my mind to see Lisa in the past few weeks, replaying scenes and speeches and incidents. Certainly Lisa wasn't getting any better. After that one therapy session where we put M.N. on, therapy meetings just melted into sitting around and talking about a lot of stuff that didn't mean anything. Didn't mean anything to Lisa, that is.

For it seemed only with me would Lisa talk about her illness. I don't know why, but Lisa loved to sit and talk at me after school. She would walk home with me and we'd sit in the game room, drinking or eating or watching television, and she'd ramble on and on.

Sometimes she would be Lisa, and sometimes

she would be her mother and talk through her teeth, which doubled me up. Sometimes she would say awful things and use terrible words, but usually in her other, English voice, when, I guess, she was someone else altogether. I guess it pleased that person, whoever she was, to shock me. She did.

She would call me names I had never even read, and she'd explain sex and physical things sometimes until I thought I'd just pass out from embarrassment. Then, other times, she'd tear me apart—being funny, I suppose she thought. Her sense of humor, which was always fast, got faster and sharper and meaner. She used it like a magician who holds up his sword to show you how sharp it is. The blade shines and everything is still. Then he picks up a piece of silk and throws it in the air above the sword. It falls gently, cut in half by simply landing on the razor-sharp edge of the sword.

Lisa loved to show off the same way, to demonstrate how clever she was, how mean and brilliant and in charge.

For example, one Friday in homeroom, we were all talking about a trip we were making the next day into a poor part of town to help clean up the neighborhood after an enormous fire. Some of the kids were nervous about it, but our teacher, who was something of a do-gooder anyway, told us not to be. What was important was that we were giving help because we wanted to. It would be a good experience for us all.

"For everyone who goes," Lisa reminded the teacher.

"Well, yes," the woman said. "For everyone who goes. Aren't you planning to come with us, Lisa?"

"Actually," Lisa said, giving us her mother's voice, "actually, I simply can't. I just haven't had time to get all my shots."

It was a set-up, of course, and it was bitter and brutal when you looked at three or four people in our class. But it was Lisa's and she loved it, and she chuckled through the rest of the hour.

For another example, one afternoon we were sitting in my house, talking about something our social sciences' teacher had brought up that day, about one's image of oneself and the image received by people looking at you. His point was that each of us was guided, to some degree, by what others thought of us, as well as by what we thought of ourselves. Lisa disagreed.

"Actually," she said, "I don't care what other people *think* of me, as long as they *see* me as I see myself." And she was off in a fit of hysterical laughter, killing herself with her own wit and falling about. I thought she was wasting a lot of good stuff on me.

But these little things happened on Lisa's good days, and those were rare. The bad days were rapidly taking over. She would begin crying for no reason in the middle of class. She was late to almost every appointment, and she was getting to be a pro about disappearing for hours at a time.

In school, she would speak out in the middle of class in her funny English voice. One line things that made no sense to any one, that seemed to come from a different girl than the one sitting there in Lisa Schilling's chair. The effect on a class when she did this was curious. There was instant silence, while everyone seemed to think about what had been said. No one looked at her. No one said anything in answer to her. The teacher would wait a minute, and then, as if nothing had happened, go on with the lesson.

There was no doubt, as I said before, that Lisa scared the hell out of us all.

I finally got to the cafeteria and spotted Elizabeth. M.N. and Lisa were at another table, already finished with their lunches. I went through the line—it was Friday; guess what we had—and then sat down with Elizabeth.

"The trouble is," I said, "Mr. Bernstein reminded me of something we forgot."

"What? I think he's done fair service with the teachers. After all, no one ever calls on Lisa now, and she always has one of us nearby."

"Well, that's just to keep her quiet. But it's nearly time for exams. That's not so bad by itself, but what happens at the end of the year?"

"How do you mean?" Elizabeth asked.

"Well, look," I explained. "You go to Maine for the summer, right? Mary Nell's whole family is going out to Ohio some place. Her father is teaching there at a summer school, and M.N.'s going along, too. *I* have a job in Westbury."

"Good grief!" Elizabeth said, startled. "You're right. I'd completely forgotten."

"Well, what are we going to do? There won't be anyone around who understands for whole months!"

Elizabeth thought a minute. "We can hope for only one thing, as far as I can see," she said.

"What?"

"That Lisa has one of her *real* sessions when she's at home, when her parents are around. Screaming is all well and good, but it's only that: screaming. If finally the Shillings see something to frighten them, they might believe the whole thing. They would have to."

"But, Elizabeth, you know they don't pay any attention to her, anyway."

"True," Elizabeth said, thinking. "Maybe there is one other, last ditch thing."

"What? What is it?"

Elizabeth looked at me a minute without smiling. "It's nothing. Never mind. It may not work, anyway," she said, her face clouding a little. It was a look I'd often seen, and it fascinated me. But I was no closer to understanding what that particular look meant than I was when I first saw it.

"I've got to go," Elizabeth said suddenly, standing up. "Do you mind finishing by yourself?"

"No. Of course not. See you."

"O.K.," she said, and turned to walk away.

I watched her go, trying to pull some hunch

95

out of my own dark recesses that could explain Elizabeth Frazer. Whatever the idea was she had, it was one that she had *not* just thought of, for Elizabeth didn't *just think* of anything. I tried to think what her idea might be, but I didn't get too far. I saw Brian Morris across the way, watching me.

He wasn't watching, exactly. It was a different look, one I couldn't remember seeing before. It was an interested stare. I was just beginning to wonder what effect my Woodward Special would have on Brian when I remembered Lisa, and her outburst at Mary Nell. Even though she said nothing could matter less to her, Lisa did still care. How could I even begin to think about Brian *that way* when I knew that?

Easy.

Well, I thought, *what the hell. Guilt could be like that approach-avoidance thing and hang you up forever. I want to live, live, live! If Joanne married gorgeous Paul, her smile must have had some effect!* So I launched it at Brian, the full one, not the warm-up I'd given Bernstein.

I let it start in my left corner, let it spread slowly upward, across my forehead, let it sink down *very* slowly until it hit the right corner of my mouth, and then held the whole beautiful thing for a full five seconds. It took a minute, but at last Brian smiled. Smiled back at *me! Cool Hand Luke*, indeed! Luke wouldn't have had a chance.

★ 16 ★

A few weeks later, on a Sunday when none of us
had anything to do, Elizabeth asked the three
of us up to her house for dinner. Her mother
had gone into New York for a few days to their
apartment, and Mr. Frazer had been in Europe
for the past few weeks, so Elizabeth was alone.
She decided we should all cook our own hamburgers on an open fire in back of their house.

It was the first time Elizabeth had ever
asked us to anything. I realized that without us,
M.N. and Lisa and me, Elizabeth's chances of
making friends would have been pretty slim.
Elizabeth was beautiful, but what seemed like
coldness in her put people off. Boys thought she
was sensational, of course, and took her out.
But nothing ever seemed to last.

Not that Elizabeth pushed them away or
anything. I guess they felt inferior, mentally, so
that after a couple of dates a guy would give up
and fall back into the crowd until someone else
took a chance.

Anyway, we arrived at about six and sat outside doing nothing for a while. It had been a
beautiful day and the evening hadn't yet

97

turned cool. Summer was definitely on its way, which raised everyone's spirits. Especially after the year we had all had. The only problem was, as I said before, what about Lisa and summertime? It was a problem we hadn't *begun* to solve.

Lisa was having what was one of her few good days left, so the talk was general, the kind of thing any girls our age would talk about. We roamed from Mama Cass to Vanessa Redgrave, from *The Graduate* to *2001* and the latest Rowan and Martin bit. From longer skirts to Elizabeth's mother's diamonds, which are huge. From Natalie Wood to *Last Summer*, and from there to drugs (largely on the basis of rumor, I'm sorry to say) to *Hair*. We even got around to civil rights and riots, but this was mostly for M.N.'s benefit, so she could hold forth for her allotted five minutes. I wanted to talk about sex, but I was hooted down in favor of Paul Newman.

Anyway, we were having a lot of fun. The hamburgers were great, and afterward Elizabeth made a new kind of instant coffee that wasn't half bad.

"Coffee drinking is like smoking," M.N. said. "It's something you do to show how old you are."

"I just like it," Lisa said. "I'd rather like it than think about it."

"But thinking separates us from animals," M.N. said. "I'm glad we can do it."

"Thinking also takes the fun out of doing," Elizabeth added.

"It's better to live than to think about living," Lisa agreed. She said it lightly, but her voice was a little deeper, a little more brittle than before. We should have paid more attention.

"On the other hand," I said, barreling in, "if you can't do something you want to, it doesn't do any real harm imagining that you're doing it."

"Oh, Betsy," Mary Nell laughed. "You're back to Paul Newman!"

"Well," I blushed, "he's certainly good at *some* things I like to think about."

"Actually," Lisa said, "this is circuitous. We're circling and getting nowhere except back again."

"True," Elizabeth said, again ignoring Lisa's new tone, hearing the "actually" but not understanding it. "I'd rather talk about anything than about talking or thinking. Let's carve someone up instead. Come on, M.N., who has what complex today?"

Mary Nell laughed and started to think who her target would be. Elizabeth went back to the fireplace and began putting out the fire. Clouds of smoke puffed up each time she shoveled sand out onto the coals. Lisa stood up and took a few steps toward Elizabeth. A cloud of smoke suddenly rose up from the fireplace, and she stopped. When it had lessened she took another step forward until she was standing directly behind Elizabeth.

That was all we saw for a minute, for another puff of smoke rose and held both Elizabeth and

Lisa in its blue-gray bounds for a second. When it cleared, I screamed, "Elizabeth!"

Lisa had shoved Elizabeth toward the dying fire, and had jumped on her in one movement. She began hitting Elizabeth's face, then changed her attack and began punching Elizabeth everywhere she could—her sides, her stomach, kicking at her legs, grabbing her by the hair. It was terrifying.

M.N. and I jumped up and ran toward the fireplace. Lisa was almost superhuman. She was a windmill, striking out in every direction, blow after blow battering Elizabeth who by now had covered her head with her arms and doubled over, more in protection I hoped than in pain. She didn't cry out or ask for help. And Lisa just kept swinging until Elizabeth sank onto the grass.

Mary Nell made a grab for Lisa, who swung around and slapped her hard across the face. M.N. recoiled, shocked, and then plunged back toward Lisa, grabbing one of her arms and reaching for the other. Lisa struck out with her legs, kicking furiously at any part of M.N. she could reach.

I ran behind Lisa, for some reason remembering what people do to horses in a fire. I waited for the right moment and then swung both arms up and over Lisa's head from behind, bringing my hands down, fingers locked together, covering her eyes. This took Lisa off balance, the weight of an attack from behind, and the temporary blindness. She lost her footing and fell backward against me.

I was scared stiff, and as she fell I naturally let go so she would fall alone. When she hit the ground, eyes open and arms still swinging, she screamed as I'd never heard anyone scream, not even in the movies. Then all was quiet.

Elizabeth got up. She had a cut lip and her hair was pulled down and hung over to one side, covering an eye that was going to be bruised for several days. She had skinned her elbows, and one was bleeding slightly. Her breath came in little gasps, as though she were trying to laugh but pain kept her from doing so.

M.N., who had only a few marks on her legs, went over to examine Elizabeth's wounds. I ran into the house to the medicine cabinet and brought back what I could find: iodine and band-aids.

Lisa, meanwhile, stayed where she'd fallen, in a sort of trance. She neither moved nor spoke. It seemed as though she wasn't even breathing. She stared straight ahead.

Mary Nell, naturally, recovered enough to get mad. "Lisa," she said, "how could you do that? Don't you understand, Elizabeth is a friend of yours? She's just like us, Betsy and me. We want to help, damn it! We can't unless you let us, you know. I don't know what makes you like this, but it has to stop. That's all there is to it!"

"Let her be," Elizabeth whispered. "She had her reasons."

"For heaven's sake," M.N. said. "That's ridiculous! We can't let her do this kind of thing

101

whenever she wants to. It's dangerous. She could have killed you."

"No," Elizabeth said slowly. "No, she wouldn't. Mary Nell, let it go. Just forget it, will you, please?"

"But Elizabeth—"

"Mary Nell! I said forget it!"

M.N. shut up.

Suddenly I thought I knew. Elizabeth had been through this before! That *had* to be it. How could she just take the awful beating Lisa gave her and then want to make excuses for it? She hadn't even fought back. She hadn't cried out. She had taken it, and waited, somehow certain Lisa would wear herself out and stop of her own accord. It was gutsy. And it could only have come from one source. Somewhere before, Elizabeth Frazer had been through it all.

And Lisa must have known. Some sign, some signal must have been exchanged between them at the very beginning, long before Lisa had gotten violent. Before any of *us*, even, knew what was happening to her, Lisa must have known and somehow Elizabeth had let her know she knew, too.

Suddenly, all I wanted to do was go home, to sit down and just be near my father, watching T.V. or reading or talking about anything in the world except this.

And so I did.

Miraculously, the next day in school Elizabeth looked as though little or nothing had happened. She had put make-up on her eye, and the cut on her lip was camouflaged with lipstick. She wore a long-sleeved blouse that covered her arms, and the only way you could tell her elbows had been hurt was by noting she never sat at her desk with them on it. She held her arms in close to her sides, as though she were holding some sort of extra pain in. I wondered if maybe Lisa had broken a couple of her ribs as well. But I didn't say anything.

From that day on, M.N. and I never left Lisa's side. We ate lunch with her. We walked her to school. We took her home with us. On weekends, one of us was always "on call" and could be free in five minutes if Lisa felt she needed us. Elizabeth had withdrawn, not because of Lisa's attack, but more to think things through.

"We have to decide what to do next," she told me. "I have to work this thing out."

"All right," I had said. "Whatever you think is best."

103

"Yes," said Elizabeth.

For some reason, I knew Lisa was relying on Elizabeth to solve her problem—not the madness, but the aloneness, the agony, the fear she felt. Because by now, Lisa was terrified of what she might do next.

"You have to promise me something," she said once to me.

"Sure," I said. "What?"

"That the next time, when I go—nuts, you won't try to handle it by yourselves. Neither you nor M.N. nor Elizabeth. I want you to call the police."

"The police! But that's awful. They won't give you the help you need."

"I know that. But they might give the news to my parents. *They* might be able to convince them where we can't. You have to promise me you'll call them, Betsy. Promise me."

"All right," I said. "I give you my word."

"Good," Lisa said, and then the light went out and she fell silent again which, by then, had become her usual state.

I told Mr. Bernstein what Lisa wanted. "She's right, I think," he said. He put his fingers together and began his little swinging motion. "You see," he went on, "*she knows*. That Shilling's a very smart girl. She sees what's happening, and she doesn't want it to. That is really very good. It means she's fighting herself herself, if you know what I mean. She still knows her from her, her old self from the new one."

"But knowing that doesn't get us anywhere.

Every day she gets worse. Even Mr. Milne said he would have to keep her out of class if she couldn't stop interrupting. Naturally, she can't."

"Well," Mr. Bernstein said, "we have something like three weeks left. Perhaps she can hold on. Then she'll have the time she needs to rest, and the responsibility will be her family's, as it should be."

"But she won't have help! She won't have us, or you, or even Mr. Milne!"

"That could be a good thing. Her parents will *have* to open their eyes."

"Oh, I hope so. How we all hope so!"

But really I wasn't hopeful. So far, the Shillings had never seen Lisa in one of her moods. She was always able, somehow, to seem more or less normal around them.

Actually, she wasn't at all able to seem one way or another at home. There was something inside her that was being held back, that the "English" side of her hid and wouldn't set free when her parents were around. It was a joke of a mean, desperate, evil kind, and it depressed all of us. God knows what it did to Lisa.

So when she was at home, Lisa ate dinner alone and then went up to her room to "do her homework." It was when she was alone that anything happened, if it did. No one else knew or saw or detected a strangeness.

Lisa's little sister Tracy, though, did call M.N. once to ask if she thought there was anything funny about the way Lisa was behaving.

"Why?" asked M.N.

"I don't know, exactly," Tracy said. "I just remember that one dinner we had, when you were there. And it seems sometimes she's not there, you know? I mean, she hardly ever says anything to me, just looks clear through me when we're together. It's scarey, is all. I thought maybe something was bothering her I didn't know about."

"What do your parents say?" M.N. asked hopefully.

"Nothing. They think everything's fine," Tracy answered.

"Oh," M.N. said. "Then I guess everything is. But Tracy—"

"Yes?"

"Nothing. Never mind. It was just an idea was all. Bye."

"What were you going to say?" I asked M.N. later.

"I don't know," she said. "I thought about asking her to come over some time when Lisa was with us."

"Well, why didn't you? Maybe *she* could persuade her parents."

"I guess because she's only twelve. It seems awful to let her see her sister like that."

"She'll have to know some time," I said. "So will her family."

"We'll let them find out by themselves," M.N. said and went back to reading *Modern Clinical Psychology*.

And I envied her. M.N., I mean. Because she was always poring over journals and magazines and those dreadful looking books with double

106

columns in tiny print, looking for answers. I guess M.N. thought she had found some. I hadn't. I was more confused every day.

Because I kept thinking about Lisa and Elizabeth at the fireplace. I couldn't understand why, if Lisa counted on Elizabeth to help her, she attacked her. If Elizabeth really had been through something like Lisa's sickness before, and if Lisa wanted help, why strike out at the one person who better than anyone else might save her? It was a strange way to go about getting help.

I finally had to settle my own mind as best I could, and all I could think was that maybe that was plain and simple what madness was: doing just the opposite of what you wanted to do, and having no control over any of it. It was a poor explanation, but I still believed that Lisa wanted our help, and I still wanted to give it.

Things were quiet for a while then. Lisa said nothing and caused no one any trouble. And a couple of times I saw her fall asleep in class, just as she had said. It was groovy!

You could hardly tell when it happened, except that her hands relaxed. She sat up straight, her eyes wide open. But her hands would sort of release themselves, and the pencil she ordinarily clutched like a talisman would slip out of her grip and roll into her lap. And that was that. She could sit that way for what seemed like hours, awakening without a start when the bell rang to change classes. It was the neatest way to go through school I'd ever seen.

Meanwhile, I was memorizing the telephone numbers of the police emergency squad, *and* the fire department, *and* an ambulance service. I figured I might as well be prepared for the worst.

But while I had promised Lisa I'd call the police if ever she went berserk again, I didn't want to. I kept hoping that when it came, if it came, it would be no worse than before. Something we *could* handle ourselves. For though I agreed that the police might be an answer to our problem, I hated the thought of showing Lisa off to outsiders. It seemed cruel and mean, and the very idea made me depressed. Still, when it did come, there was nothing else to do but use a special number. I just had to.

★ **18** ★

Our therapy sessions with Lisa by this time had taken on definite form. There was no therapy offered at all, except our own presence when Lisa wanted it. She had stopped trying to explain what was happening in her head. She no longer told about her fears or about her wonderment when the "thing" came on her. She wouldn't even talk about how important it was for her parents to know and admit she was ill.

M.N. informed us that Lisa was in a precatatonic stage. This meant that she had become emotionless, with neither the desire to live or speak normally. That all we could expect from here on in was silence, immobility, a zombie, in fact. (I used that word once and M.N. nearly killed me. Not because it sounded unkind toward Lisa, but because it wasn't scientific.)

I wasn't quite ready to give Lisa up yet. Mostly because I didn't feel the same way Mary Nell did about her silences. They could be broken when *she* wanted to break them.

One night after school we were all at my house. My parents had gone out to an early dinner, and my brother was messing around somewhere up the street, so we had the house to ourselves. Which wasn't that exciting since all we did was sit around. Elizabeth and I would talk about this or that, and M.N. had a book open on her lap from which she would read when the talk wasn't as exciting as she liked.

Lisa was in her usual spot, sitting on the floor, cross-legged, hunched over, listening or not as the mood took her. She was, by that time, several pounds thinner than she had ever been. And you could tell that when she was at home, sleep wasn't anything that interested her any more than food. Her eyes had dark circles under them and her face was drawn tight against the outside world.

Once in a while, Elizabeth or I would ask Lisa a question, hoping to break through to find out that she could still talk. But she ignored us, never even raising her head when we spoke. Sometimes she would nod yes or no, but not in answer to what we were saying. It seemed there was someone inside her who was carrying on a very serious, very long and detailed conversation with her, and these nods were her way of speaking whole volumes with the least possible effort. Whoever it was inside apparently understood.

So there we were—Fickett, Frazer, Goodman, and Shilling—one night after school. We had made peanut-butter sandwiches (dietetic peanut-butter, naturally) and had some warm consommé, and were trying to decide what to watch on television. There was a fairly good movie on (*Rally 'Round the Flag, Boys!* with my baby Paul), but we decided against it because it would have kept us all up later than we wanted. There wasn't much else on except some educational stuff and a game show, which we all hate.

Suddenly, the door from the hallway opened and there was my father, back much too early from dinner. "Hi, girls," he said, walking straight into the room.

I may have forgotten to mention that outside of M.N.'s father, none of our parents knew about Lisa. It was sort of stupid, maybe, but we decided that if Mr. Fickett had struck out so easily, my father probably wouldn't do that much better and Elizabeth's father was in Europe too often to even try.

Anyway, there was my father, walking right in. I guess there was no reason for him not to, considering it was his house, too. Both Elizabeth and I stood up and moved in front of Lisa as M.N. began talking to him, hoping somehow to be polite and yet tell him to go away.

"Hi, Mr. Goodman," M.N. said. "Where's Mrs. Goodman?"

"I think she's in the kitchen, Mary Nell. Is there something you want?"

"Oh no, not really," M.N. answered. "I just thought I heard her calling you, is all."

"You did?" Father said.

"Probably just my imagination," M.N. admitted.

"Probably," Father agreed.

"Hello, Mr. Goodman," Lisa said.

Elizabeth and I whirled around. Lisa was sitting up straight and smiling!

"Well, hello, Lisa," Father said, peering over the couch past M.N. to speak to her. "How are you?"

"I'm fine, thank you," Lisa said, standing up. She was still smiling.

Father looked at her a moment, but she didn't say anything more. "Well," he said, "I'm glad to hear that."

"Yes," Lisa said for no reason.

Then she turned around, toward the wall of glass that looked out on to our backyard. Still smiling, she went toward the windows. We could see her reflection from head to foot, and she must have seen it, too, for it was dark outside then and you couldn't possibly mistake the glass for no glass, if you know what I mean.

But that's what Lisa did. Or that's the way

111

it seemed, anyway. She stepped up to the wall of glass and walked right through it. Her right foot went through first with an unearthly shattering sound, and then her whole right leg. Then her body pushed the break, head down, and she was through! "Lisa!" M.N. screamed. "Good God!" cried Father, running after her.

But Lisa just kept walking. She stopped, finally, and turned to face us. Her head was streaming blood and her leg had a line of blood streaking down and running out into the grass. She was still smiling.

"I'm fine, thank you," she said. Then she fainted.

We all sprang into action. Father rushed out into the yard, taking off his jacket and slipping it under her head. Elizabeth took off her blouse (guts, that girl!) and followed, tearing it into strips to stop the flow of blood. I grabbed the telephone and dialed a number I had memorized.

M.N. dashed into the kitchen for some toweling and was back in a flash at Lisa's side, cleaning the wounds.

"Betsy!" called my father. "Call the Shillings. Get them over here."

"O.K., Dad," I said and turned back to the phone, trembling. This would be it. Lisa had an adult witness now and her parents couldn't help but see her now as we did.

"Hello, Mrs. Shilling? Is your husband home? Oh. Well," I said, taking a deep breath, "then I guess you had better get over here. Where? The

112

Goodman's house," I said. "This is Betsy Goodman."

Naturally she wanted to know why, since her
husband was out of town. "There's been a sort
of accident, Mrs. Shilling," I said. "Lisa is pretty bloody." I *loved* telling her *that!* She gasped
and said she was on her way. At least *that*
much had gotten through to her.

By that time Lisa was bandaged as well as
she could be and covered with one of Father's
coats. Elizabeth and M.N. stayed at her side as
my father walked back in.

"The ambulance should be here in a minute,"
I told him.

"She knew exactly what she was doing," Father said shaking his head. "What the hell is
the matter with her?"

"She's very sick, Dad," I said. "Really. In her
mind."

"Mr. Goodman!" M.N. called from the
backyard. Father turned around and ran out.
I followed and we looked down at Lisa whose
eyes were flickering. She opened them fully and
looked up at Father. She smiled at him. "Thank
you," she said. Then she sank back into her
unconsciousness.

Father stood there shaking his head, puzzled. Elizabeth stood up. "Mr. Goodman," she
said, "you may have saved Lisa's life."

"I don't understand," Father said. "I don't
understand at all."

"Lisa needed you," Elizabeth told him, not
even thinking about the cold or the night or
the fact that she had no blouse on. "Her own

113

family has never seen she needs help. Now *you* have."

"What does she want from me?" asked Father.

"You have to tell Mrs. Shilling, Dad," I said. "She wouldn't listen to any of us, but she will to you."

"After all," M.N. added, "what kind of girl would purposely walk through a wall of glass? It's suicide."

"Someone who badly needed help, I guess," Father admitted and turned back into the house as he heard the ambulance siren.

Within seconds, four white-coated doctors and attendants were in the backyard, administering to Lisa. They covered her up nearly to her head and lifted her on to a stretcher so gently that you couldn't believe it. They were carrying her through the house when Mrs. Shilling walked in.

"What happened!" she shouted. "Where are you taking her?"

"To Mount Cedar," one of the attendants said. "She'll be all right. Do you want to ride in the ambulance with her?"

Mrs. Shilling turned white. "No!" she said. "No, I'll drive myself."

"Yes, ma'am," the man said. They carried Lisa out to the car and loaded her into the back of it. The siren sounded before the car moved and then they all took off, red lights and siren and speed all blurring into the night.

"Will someone please tell me what exactly

114

happened here?" Mrs. Shilling said through her teeth, staring at Elizabeth as an afterthought.

"Come in and rest a minute," said Father, taking her arm and leading her into the game room. "I'm sure Lisa will be fine. This," he said pointing to the nonexistent window, "is what happened."

"What? Did someone push her?"

"No," Father said. "She walked through it."

"What!" Mrs. Shilling gasped. "She walked through it?"

"Yep," M.N. said. "Just ducked her head and dove through."

"But there must have been a reason. What was happening? What were you doing to her?" Mrs. Shilling wanted to know.

"Mrs. Shilling," Father said, "sit down, won't you, for just a moment."

She did, but she wasn't happy. "Well?"

"Well," said Father, "it seems you have a very sick girl on your hands."

"What do you mean?"

"I'm not sure, really," Father admitted. "I guess she's upset, and feels she needs help from someone."

"What it is, Mrs. Shilling," M.N. said, "is that Lisa is slowly losing her mind, and she's scared to death. *You* haven't paid any attention to it, or to her, so when she saw Mr. Goodman she walked through the glass to prove it."

"That's absurd!" Mrs. Shilling said, standing up. "You've tried twice to tell us Lisa is going crazy. It's your doing, Mary Nell. Your imagination is working overtime. There's nothing wrong with Lisa except a little tension about schoolwork. The school psychologist told us that long ago."

"This is a fairly extreme way of indicating tension," Elizabeth said.

"Obviously," Mrs. Shilling said, "you're making all this up. It must have been an accident of some kind, that's all. No one in his right mind would purposely do something like this."

"Exactly," said Elizabeth.

"Mrs. Shilling," Father said quietly. "Would it do any harm to let a professional see her? I mean, just in case what the girls say *is* true."

"Are you mad?" Mrs. Shilling answered. "There's nothing at all wrong with Lisa that a little discipline won't cure. She's simply a spoiled selfish girl who is showing off for some absurd reason. We have no intention of letting her ride roughshod over us."

"Mrs. Shilling," Elizabeth said, moving closer to her. "I'm going to tell you something once. Whether you listen or not is your affair."

"Now you be careful, Elizabeth Frazer. I'm not going to take any smart talk from some sixteen-year-old bitch-to-be!"

Wow! I thought. *Just wow!*

"Mrs. Shilling," Elizabeth said as cold as ice. "Your daughter is sick. If you don't admit it, she may have to spend the rest of her life in an institution. She needs your help, *now!* Give it to her, and stop thinking about yourself for just one fraction of a second. Take a look at Lisa. She is screaming for help!"

116

Mrs. Shilling looked at Elizabeth a second, and then swung out with her right hand and slapped her across the face. Elizabeth took the blow without flinching and then, not even blinking, flashed out and clipped Mrs. Shilling right back! Wowee!!!

"Elizabeth," Father said.

But Elizabeth had already turned away from the astonished Mrs. Shilling and was putting on her sweater.

"Now you listen to me!" Mrs. Shilling screamed suddenly. "You're doing this to her! It's your work, you girls! I don't want any of you, ever, to come near Lisa again! Is that clear? You're to stay away or I'll have every one of you put away! If you dare go near that hospital, or try to call her, I'll have you all put behind bars! My God! Oh, my God!" and she ran out of the room, jumped into her car and roared off.

You can imagine how depressed we were, then, for the next few days. With Lisa in the hospital, since we weren't able to visit her (my parents were very firm about *that*), there didn't seem to be anything to do. We had exams staring at us, of course, so the three of us buckled down harder I think than we would have otherwise to forget our own anxieties.

The thing was, I don't think any of us realized how one-sided we had become during the past few months. We had concentrated so hard on Lisa and on trying to do what we could for her, that we had nearly forgotten there was a world without this kind of sickness. A world where we were supposed to be having the time of our lives, a world without huge responsibilities and problems—our "golden days."

But none of this seemed as important as what we were doing. And at which, it finally seemed, we had failed. But good! After all we had tried to do, after all Lisa had tried to do herself, she was still no closer to getting help. That she *was* closer to finally smashing up was only too clear.

It was very, very depressing.

I spent as much time as I could with my father. I told him what had been happening, how we had first seen Lisa's illness and tried to diagnose it. How we had decided her only help would come from us, and how badly we'd failed.

My father said he wasn't sure yet we had failed. After all, he said, we still didn't know what the Shillings were going to do. Perhaps Lisa's plunge had made the difference. He hoped so. So did I. And I was very grateful he was my Dad and not Mr. Shilling, wherever he still was.

My mother, too, tried to be as helpful as she could. She had the window repaired the next day, and invited M.N. and Elizabeth over for dinner outdoors. She said this was all a lot like riding a horse—if you were thrown, you just had to get back up to show the horse you weren't afraid. Still and all, the three of us weren't the most stimulating dinner companions. We couldn't think of anything but Lisa and the sound of glass smashing, and the non-sound of streaking blood.

M.N., of course, was the first to recover and be her old self. She was full of optimism about everything. She told us how it was a state law that if a hospital discovered a suicide attempt, it had to assign a psychiatrist to the person who had tried it. (I tried to persuade my father to call the hospital, then, but he wouldn't.) And that maybe, while she was in the hospital, Lisa would reach out to a doctor or a nurse, and find someone to believe her.

Elizabeth and I, though, were rather suspended for a time. We went to school and took tests and passed them simply because we had nothing to do but study for them. It was a good thing, probably, but it hurt anyway. We missed Lisa whether sick or well. She had become more than someone who needed help to us. She had become a full-time occupation.

And then one day Elizabeth didn't show up for school. Although neither M.N. nor I thought too much about it, we called her anyway at lunchtime. Her mother said Elizabeth wasn't ill, just taking the day off to run an important errand.

"Well," M.N. said, "that's reasonable. Something probably came up that had to be done right away."

"What, I wonder," I said. "Besides, she's missing an hour exam in calculus."

"Elizabeth's a pretty fair student," M.N. reminded me. "Miss Strane will let her make it up."

Still, I thought to myself. I couldn't think of any kind of errand that would keep *me* out of school. A doctor's appointment or something, maybe, but surely Elizabeth's mother would have told us that if it were true. There was nothing I could do, and no reason to worry, but I did.

The thing was, I was still in awe of Elizabeth Frazer. Since I discovered what I thought sure I had discovered, I mean that she had had *some* experience with this type illness before, I was *very* impressed. Maybe what Elizabeth knew about wasn't exactly Lisa's kind of thing, but somehow Elizabeth had strength and knowledge and a determination that made her confident and secure in handling Lisa that could only have come from having handled someone else the same way.

I didn't mention any of this to M.N. who would have badgered the life out of Elizabeth to find out what, and when, and where and who and most of all, probably, why. For not only was M.N. the hungriest reader of all time, when she was on the trail of something she was more determined than a Mountie. With her nose down and her eyes up, M.N. would follow tracks until she faced her quarry brow-to-brow. Whatever she had been hunting had no chance. Once M.N. has the advantage, she never loses it. She is the world's number one nose.

Anyway, I worried about Elizabeth, but maybe it was only because I was worried about everything then. Happily, there was one time— for just a few minutes—when I couldn't worry, for as M.N. and I walked into the cafeteria one day, there *he* was. He, of course, is you know who—the recipient of my famous, although a little guilty, Joanne Woodward smile.

As we came out of the line and walked toward an empty table, Brian and I locked eyes. Eye-contact, we call it: E.C. I felt sort of hot, suddenly, and I couldn't hold his look. I hadn't been prepared for something like that that day. Besides, you can't just leap into a Woodward Special with no preparation, no warm-up time.

But *he* smiled. I nodded and grinned back a little, the old stand-by grin that Betsy Goodman uses in moments of stress. It is spectacularly dreary. But it didn't stop Brian Morris.

I ducked my head as he came over. "Hi," he said.

"Hi, Bri," M.N. said.

"Hello," I muttered.

"I hear Lisa went home this morning," he said. This was news to us.

"How do you know?" M.N. asked.

"My brother. He's an intern at Cedar," Brian explained.

"Did you go to visit?" I asked.

"No," Brian said. "I thought about it, but I couldn't do it."

121

"Probably just as well," said M.N. positively. "What she needs is a visit of another kind anyway."

Brian looked at M.N. a minute, puzzled, and then decided to let it go. "See you," he said to me.

"Bye," I said. And it made me furious to have him just walk away like that. It was all M.N.'s fault. She had made both of us nervous. Then I smiled a little. I reminded myself of Mrs. Shilling, blaming the first person who came into sight for something she herself controlled. Oh well.

Elizabeth wasn't in school the next day, either. I decided to stop worrying. If no one else was, why should I? That's what I decided. I worried anyway.

At dinner that night the telephone rang.

"It's for you," my brother told me.

I excused myself and went into the hall. "Hello?"

"Betsy? Elizabeth."

"Oh, hi," I said, struggling not to say "where have you been?"

"Listen," Elizabeth said quickly, "can you come out here after dinner tonight?"

"I suppose so," I said. "What's up?"

"You'll see when you get here. M.N.'s coming over, too."

I felt better as I hung up the phone and went back into the dining room. Elizabeth was back. Even if I never found out where she'd been, at least she'd come back.

And then I wondered what was going on. It

122

had to be something about Lisa, but what? I gave up trying to guess, because I had recently begun to suspect that every time you expect one thing from life, something else usually happens. There was no point in being constantly disappointed.

But that was the last thing in the world I was when I got to Elizabeth's house—disappointed, I mean.

★ 20 ★

M.N. got there ahead of me and when Elizabeth opened the door, I could hear her holding forth to someone else in the living room.

"Hi, Betsy," Elizabeth said, greeting me with the happiest smile I'd ever seen on her face.

"Hi," I said.

"There's someone here I want you to meet, and who wants to meet you," Elizabeth said as we walked into her living room.

And there he was! Oh good grief, ohgoodgriefgoodgrief, there he was! Farewell Paul Newman! Farewell forever dear, dear Paul! Forgive me! It's bigger than both of us! I can't help myself! Farewell Paul Baby and hello, hello, hello Neil Donovan!

For that was his name. Elizabeth introduced us, and that was his name! I couldn't breathe for a minute, not even enough to say hello politely. I think I was in shock. My own precatatonic state. I just stood there and stared at Neil Donovan, whoever he was.

He was about six feet tall, maybe more, with long, wavy sandy hair that fell over his forehead a little and curled up at the back of his neck. He had what has got to be the most beautiful nose in the world. It was like the old Greek noses—aquiline is the word, I think. (Actually, maybe aquiline was the Roman nose. Oh well.) What I mean is a thin nose, running down with a bump and a curve, that looks as though someone carved it from stone.

And his eyes! Dear heart, his eyes! Paul's are keen and all but they're also three thousand miles away or on a huge screen. Neil's were right there, in front of me, *looking* at me! They were even brighter and clearer and bluer than Paul's and "oh" was all I could ever have said looking into them.

I must have looked like an idiot for Elizabeth touched my elbow and moved me farther into the room. "Neil is an old friend of mine," she said as he sat down again. "We met nearly four years ago, and we've been close friends ever since."

I began to recover as Elizabeth placed me gently in a chair. At least recovered enough to see M.N., sitting on the *same couch* as Neil, look at me and smile. I smiled back to say "hi." Then I looked at *him* again. He *was* beautiful, but he was also maybe thirty-seven or thirty-eight. *Oh well,* I thought, *stranger things have happened.*

"Neil's an analyst," Elizabeth said. "A psychiatrist. I asked him to stop by so we could talk about Lisa and figure out some way to help her finally."

"Yes," Neil Donovan said to me. "I wanted to talk to Mary Nell, here, and to you, Betsy. I thought if you both told me what you know about Lisa that with that and with what Elizabeth's already told me, I could form some sort of picture of her. Then, together, we may be able to reach her."

"Together?" I managed to ask. "Don't psychiatrists work alone?"

"Yes, they do," he said. "But in this case, since you have all worked so hard with Lisa already, I think it's only fair to be working *with* you, rather than after you."

"Neil and M.N. are going to start, Betsy," Elizabeth said. "We can go into the library while they're talking. Come on."

I resisted the impulse to have to be dragged away and got up docilely to follow Elizabeth from the room. I wondered what effect Joanne Woodward would have on Neil Donovan and decided to save that until later.

"Elizabeth!" I whispered when we were in the library. "Who *is* he? I've never seen anyone so absolutely technicolor!"

Elizabeth laughed. "He's just an old friend, Betsy, really, and he came because I asked him to, to help us."

125

"Is that why you were away?" I couldn't help asking.

"Yes, it is. He lives upstate."

"Elizabeth," I said, "if I ask you a question will you promise not to get mad?"

"What's the question?" Elizabeth wanted to know.

"Did *you* live ... upstate ... before you came here?"

Elizabeth smiled, which surprised me a little. "Yes, I did."

"Is he—I mean, was he—*your* doctor?" There! It was out!

Elizabeth looked at me a minute and then nodded yes. "But don't tell M.N.," she said. "I don't think she'd ever let me be if she found out."

"No, of course I won't," I said. "You know something? I'm glad you told me."

"I'm glad you asked, Betsy. I don't know why, exactly, but I am."

"Will you, some other time, tell me about it?" I asked. "I mean, if you ever happen to feel like it."

"Perhaps," Elizabeth said. "I've never talked to anyone about that time except my parents, of course. Maybe I should."

"Well, only if you feel like it."

"We'll see."

I felt very close to Elizabeth then and, finally, I knew why. The confidence I thought she'd had was a kind of fear of us all. She had seemed distant in order to maintain her distance. The only thing she was certain of, and had been all

126

the way through, was that she alone knew how sick Lisa was because she herself had been ill. It was something she knew and wanted no one else to know. At least, not until then.

"Elizabeth, was your illness the same as Lisa's?"

"No, it wasn't. But I saw people like Lisa there. Lisa's not a new experience for me."

"Is that why she went after you that one time, because she knew you knew?"

"I don't know, Betsy. Maybe. Maybe it was just another way of crying out for help."

"Wow!" I said. "Just wow!"

"Want something to drink?" Elizabeth asked, walking over to a bar.

"O.K."

"What we have to do now," she said, "is figure how to get Neil to Lisa and then—and this is the real job—to persuade the Shillings that Lisa is sick, can be cured, and must be allowed treatment."

I took the glass of soda. "How?" I asked. "I mean, we can't even talk to Lisa any more, unless she comes back to school."

"True, but maybe something else will happen. Although I'm not sure what that would be," she said sadly.

"Elizabeth? Doesn't a psychiatrist cost a lot of money?"

"Yes. Why?"

"Well, here this gorgeous creature is, waiting to get to Lisa and talking to us instead. I'm sure it helps to find out what you can about your patient and all, but who's paying for all this?"

"My father," Elizabeth answered.

"*Your* father!"

"Yes. As a sort of favor to me. When Daddy came back from Europe, I told him everything that had happened. I have a rather extraordinary man for a father, Betsy."

"I guess so!"

"Anyway, it wasn't difficult for him to remember when I was sick. And he agreed that Lisa should have help now, even if her own family was unwilling to give it to her. I'll pay him back, of course, as soon as I can."

"This sounds silly, Elizabeth," I said, "but *you* are extraordinary. But how long can Dr. Donovan stay?"

"Not very long, I'm afraid. I'm hoping he can meet Lisa before he has to go back. But he'll come back, I know he will."

"He *is* heaven! Is it true a lot of patients fall in love with their doctors? I'd love to be a patient of his!"

"Oh Betsy," Elizabeth laughed. "I'm so very, very glad we're friends!"

There was a knock on the library door. "Come in," called Elizabeth.

It was M.N. "Your turn," she said to me. "Dr. Donovan wants to talk to you now, Betsy."

I walked out of the library and down the hall, practicing my Woodward Special. After all, it couldn't do any harm to try. It's a nice smile all by itself, even if you aren't seducing someone.

I stopped on the threshold of the living room and coughed a little. He turned around. Zap!!! I sent it across the thirty feet between us like lightning. He smiled back, but only casually. I walked in racking my brain for something I'd seen Elizabeth Taylor or Cher or Marlo Thomas use with more success.

"Sit down, Betsy," he said to me. I picked the same spot on the couch M.N. had had. He, the rat, selected a chair across from me.

"I hope you're not so well read as Mary Nell is," he said still smiling. "I've a feeling I need a refresher course in psychological terminology."

I laughed a little—a husky, sexy little chuckle à la Paula Prentiss. "No," I said, "we've left the dictionary and research to M.N. exclusively. Elizabeth and I felt that one expert was enough in this crowd."

I suddenly wished I'd had a cigarette. I don't smoke, of course, but it would have given me something to do with my hands. I could have relaxed with it, crossed my legs, and looked older blowing smoke through my nose.

"Where would you like to start?" Dr. Donovan asked.

"Well, I'm not sure. I imagine M.N. told you everything pretty clearly. She's nothing if not objective."

"Well then," he went on, "is there something that especially bothers you?"

"The whole thing *bothers* me!" I said sharply. "I mean, well, what happens next? Suppose

129

walking through glass didn't hit her family? What does she have to do, for Pete's sake?"

"You think she'll be forced to do something else? To think of something more?"

"Wouldn't you think so?" I said. "You're the expert here, not me."

Dr. Donovan stopped to think. So did I.

I was furious at myself. Here was this absolutely socko guy, and I was being as rude as I could possibly be. Not rude, really, just touchy. I guess it was because I knew my Woodward Special had failed, and that it would have failed no matter what its voltage. I would just have to take Dr. Neil Donovan at face value (gasp!) and accept him as I would anyone else, a guy who happened to be a doctor. Nothing more. (Paul! Paul! I'm back, I'm back! I'll always love you, Paul Newman! Always!)

"Suicide," Dr. Donovan said quietly. "Is that what you think?"

"Yes, I guess so," I said. "And what we have to do is get over there and stop it."

"Unfortunately, it's not quite as easy as that," Donovan said. "We can't walk in, unasked, and cart Lisa away from her family."

"It's either that," I said strongly, surprising myself, "or watch as someone in white walks in, called for, and does exactly the same thing."

21

But there wasn't much any of us could do honestly. Lisa was at home, beyond our reach and, no doubt, beyond the reach of anything else. M.N., Elizabeth, and I worried but it was wasted energy, really, since all we were left with was sitting on our hands.

Dr. Donovan, though, went around quickly and quietly researching. He spent one full day at school talking with Lisa's teachers and with Mr. Bernstein. I would like to have heard this particular conversation because, as far as I could tell, while I liked Mr. Bernstein and sympathized with him, it seemed to me that he should go up to Donovan's hospital along with Lisa and iron out *his* problems. I think what Mr. Bernstein should have been was some kind of administrator, or a computer technician, so he wouldn't have to meet *people* and deal with them directly.

That same evening Dr. Donovan came to our house to talk with Daddy who really couldn't tell him anything we hadn't already. Except, of course, Daddy's point of view being more mature it probably carried more weight than our own.

The next morning, at breakfast with Elizabeth, Neil Donovan came across something in the newspaper that interested him. "Elizabeth," he said, "how does this sound to you? Could it be your friend? 'The teen-age daughter of a near-by Sikhanout family was treated last night in Mount Cedar Hospital for an overdose of barbiturates. The youngster, whose name was not released, will recover.' "

"I don't know," said Elizabeth. "It could be Lisa. But it's indefinite. Is there some way you could find out through the hospital?"

"I can telephone," said Donovan getting up to do so. He was gone only a few minutes and came directly back to the table. "It turns out," he said, "that that *was* Lisa."

"Oh, no!" said Elizabeth.

"I'll try to find out who the consulting analyst is, because this time there will be one. By the time you get back from school we'll have some idea of what really happened."

"Why must it take that long?" Elizabeth asked. "It's just another phone call."

"Never mind. I'll tell you what," he said, "come home at lunch if you like."

"Well, at least that's better," Elizabeth had told him.

"Can I go with you?" I asked Elizabeth later that morning during a break.

"Me, too," M.N. said. "I don't see what good two of us will do without the third."

"The thing is," Elizabeth said thoughtfully,

"I don't know what good any of us is able to do. The question is, do the Shillings finally understand?"

"I can find out," I offered.

"How?" asked M.N.

"I'll have my father call. After all, Mrs. Shilling doesn't want anything to do with *us*, but Father is different. I'll call right away."

So I did. And I waited in the phone booth for Daddy to call me back—the longest four minutes thirty-seven seconds ever! Finally the phone rang. I had it in less than a second. "Hello? Daddy?"

"Yes, Betsy. I don't want to get your hopes up," he said, "but I would say that the Shillings are going to be more receptive now. Mrs. Shilling wasn't able to talk but her husband wants to meet me for coffee in forty-five minutes. He wants to know exactly what happened at our house that night, and what I think he can do."

"Oh, Daddy!" I nearly cried. "Tell him we already have found help for Lisa! Tell him about Dr. Donovan!"

"I will, Bets, don't worry. I will. See you later, O.K.?"

"O.K., Daddy, and thank you."

"It's O.K., Bets. Bye."

"Bye."

I was late getting back into Miss Strane's class but I managed a thumbs-up sign as I came in to Elizabeth and M.N., and when we broke for the next class I told them what Father had said.

"Well," said M.N., "at last! Hallelujah!"

133

"But we still have to reach Mrs. Shilling," I mentioned.

"No, we don't," Elizabeth said. "*Mr.* Shilling has to do that. If he's this close now, after he talks with your father he'll be in it all the way. She won't have a chance."

"You know what?" M.N. said. "I feel sort of sorry for her. Not that she deserves it, mind you. But it must be hell realizing one of your kids is crazy."

Elizabeth looked at M.N., strong and straight and with no smile. "Would you say it was as hard as realizing that people are human, Mary Nell? That they are single things with their own problems that won't be solved by someone else's determination?"

Mary Nell's face drained. Her eyes began to water. Elizabeth waited, unyielding. "That's not unfair," Mary Nell said slowly. "Ignore the tears." She drew in a big breath and faced Elizabeth squarely. "Yes, I would say that," she said. And then she smiled tentatively.

Elizabeth smiled back, stepped forward, and kissed M.N. very quickly on the cheek.

We all rushed to Elizabeth's house at lunch and nearly raped Dr. Donovan for news. (I looked that up. It means "to seize," which is perfectly O.K. in this sense.)

"It's not as bad as it sounded," he told us. "Lisa got hold of her mother's sleeping pills, took a handful, and walked downstairs. She lay on the couch in the living room so that when her parents came home they would find her. Which is exactly what they did. Dr. Brody, who admitted her, said he thought the parents were pretty shaken. So, between that and the talk he had with Mr. Goodman this morning, Mr. Shilling may finally be ready for us."

"The question is, how do we do it, gently?" Elizabeth asked.

"Dr. Brody said he thought if we wanted to visit Lisa later this afternoon it wouldn't do any harm."

"All of us?" I asked.

"I don't see why not," Neil said. "After all, someone will have to introduce me to my new patient."

"But what about her mother?" M.N. objected. "She was dead serious about keeping us away from Lisa."

"I don't think she'll be so firm about that now," Dr. Donovan said. "But I'll talk to Mr. Shilling before we go."

M.N. slapped her forehead. "If anything goes wrong now," she said, "you may as well forget Lisa and take me back with you!"

"I'll pick you all up after school, after your last class," said Donovan.

So we went back to school for the slowest afternoon in the history of man. We were terrifically excited. I realized that we had begun to assume that not only would Lisa be glad to see us, but she would also have miraculously recovered her mind. We expected to walk in and have her leap out of bed running open-armed for us all, laughing and chattering and free as she used to be.

But Elizabeth tried to quiet us. "We haven't

seen her in days and days," she said. "Who knows what else has happened to her, inside? It could be we've lost her totally without knowing it."

We thought about that for a moment, but dismissed it almost as fast. We simply didn't want to believe there was even a chance that we were too late, that keeping Lisa afloat until help came had been futile after all.

So, although we had been warned, we couldn't help ourselves. We tried to keep our expectations low, but it was no use. When Dr. Donovan picked us up, we were all three nearly hysterical with happiness and anticipation.

This ended as soon as we got into the hospital. No hospital in the world smells different from the hospital you learned to hate as a kid, and this one was no exception. Our eagerness shrank to nothing as we remembered all the things we'd seen Lisa do and say and go through. By the time the elevator stopped on her floor, no one wanted to get out.

"Well, come on, girls," Dr. Donovan said. "This is it. This is what you've worked so hard for. You're not going to let me go in alone, are you?"

Elizabeth was the first to follow him, and then M.N. and I stepped out and walked down the hall after them.

We stood for a minute outside Lisa's room listening. There was absolutely nothing to hear. I began to hope she wasn't even there. But then a nurse came out, nodded, and motioned for us to go in. It was M.N. who got up enough nerve to push through the door. We could see Lisa was there, after all.

She was lying in bed looking up at the ceiling. She hardly moved and if you had asked me, she could have been dead for all the motion in her body. M.N. walked closer. Elizabeth and I followed. Lisa didn't move.

"Lisa?" M.N. whispered. "Lisa? It's us. M.N. and Betsy and Elizabeth."

Lisa let her head fall to one side and looked at M.N. without seeming to recognize her.

"Hi," M.N. said.

Lisa didn't even blink!

I looked at Elizabeth. *We're too late!* I thought. *We are too late!*

Elizabeth was silent. Then she stepped up to the bedside. "Lisa," she said, "I've brought you a friend."

Lisa shifted her look from M.N. to Elizabeth.

"He's a friend of *mine*," Elizabeth emphasized. "I think perhaps he can help you, if you want him to," she said. "I think he's what we've been looking for all this time."

Elizabeth motioned from behind her back for Dr. Donovan to come in, which he did very quietly. He walked forward and stopped at Elizabeth's side, looking down over her shoulder at Lisa.

"Lisa," Elizabeth said, "this is Dr. Donovan. Dr. Donovan, this is Lisa Shilling."

Dr. Donovan gave Lisa one of his unbelievably gorgeous smiles and reached out for her hand. He took it very gently and held it a minute. "I'm very glad," he said quietly, "finally to meet you, Lisa."

Lisa looked up at Dr. Donovan for a long moment, and then back at Elizabeth. Elizabeth nodded yes to her, "it's all right," and Lisa looked back up into Dr. Donovan's face. And then a tear fell, just one. And then another, and then, without moving still, a whole torrent started.

M.N. and I started to cry, too, then, with relief and joy and who knows what else. We reached out and touched Lisa's shoulder, and each kissed her on the cheek. And then we left. We just had to. We couldn't stand around there getting hysterical.

Elizabeth came out and found us, arms around each other, in front of the elevator. She punched a button and, after a minute, we all got into the car and rode down to the street.

We ran through the lobby like three idiot children and burst through the doors. There is a little park on the side of the hospital, and we scrambled to reach it, all three of us holding hands and laughing, and crying, and giggling, and acting like three-year-olds together. And we didn't stop. We fell about in the grass, and rolled over each other, and shrieked and hooted and hollered and hit each other and then started all over again. And to think, I remembered, that the *patient* was still *inside*.

22

School ended then soon afterward, and Lisa stayed at the hospital for another week beyond even that. Not that she needed to be watched so much as it was to give her a chance to rest before going up to the hospital where Dr. Donovan worked. And this was the Shillings' idea!

For Mr. and Mrs. Shilling had, at last, been beaten down. Their resistance, their objections, their fears had all given way finally to concern that they might lose their daughter to a kind of living death far worse than any sudden cutting off naturally might have been.

Mrs. Shilling, especially, reacted. She hid at home twenty-four hours a day, never venturing outside to go to the store or the bank or even with the garbage. She felt, and you could sympathize a *little*, that every time she showed her face her neighbors were criticizing her. After all, we're told illnesses like this don't just happen. There must be reasons and background and incidents that build up to a point of tautness until a personality finds a way of releasing its tension. And Lisa's release had been in madness, plain and simple. Which, of course, if you wanted to, could be traced in part at least to her family and the way in which she had been raised.

That wasn't important to *us*, though. It mattered less what the causes were than whether Lisa would recover. "I think," Dr. Donovan had said before he left, "that Lisa may be back with you by Christmas."

I counted very fast: seven months. It was hard to believe.

"I don't mean," he said then, "that she'll be back with you full time, as good as new, ready for action as before. I mean that if we work very hard, from the minute Lisa gets settled up north, right through summer and next fall, she may be home for a visit then."

The following weekend, as the Shillings drove Lisa to the hospital and just before he left, Neil Donovan talked with us again. "This is going to sound impossible, girls, but the worst is yet to come."

M.N. slapped her forehead. "Make three more reservations, quick!" she shouted.

"You were lucky this time," Donovan said. "Lucky your other friends treated Lisa so fairly when she was alone. That isn't usual, you know."

"What would you expect?" Mary Nell asked. "After all, Lisa *was* sick. They could see it, too."

"I know," the doctor said. "And, believe me, it's remarkable that cruelty and easy fun didn't occur to anyone. It will."

"Why?" I asked. "When Lisa comes back full

140

time, she'll be just like the rest of us. Won't she?"

"Yes, but she'll be more sensitive, too. It's not easy not to make fun of someone who's just come out of a . . . a nuthouse."

Elizabeth started to object but Donovan cut her off. "I know that sounds harsh, Elizabeth, but it's true. We all know how easy a target someone who's been ill is. Your job, all of your jobs, is going to be very tough indeed. Not to insulate Lisa but to educate the others."

This, of course, was right up M.N.'s alley. "Well, then," she said, "maybe you could write to us every so often. Keep us up-to-date so we *can* educate everybody here."

"Poor M.N.," Elizabeth laughed. "You've had a chance to study everything but the patient's mind. I hate to think of all that reading and no primary source available to you. Maybe Neil could send bulletins."

"If there is time," Neil Donovan said seriously, "I will."

"As long as it doesn't take time away from Lisa," M.N. said quickly. "Or your other patients."

"Right," he said, and smiled.

"I have learned *so* much," M.N. said. Elizabeth smiled.

"So have I," I offered. "What I'll do with it all, though, I don't know."

"There's no rush to put all your information and all your good intent to work," Donovan said. "You'll have years and years yet to do

141

that. But maybe you'd like to come up and visit our hospital during the summer."

"I can't," M.N. said sadly. "I'll be in Ohio."

"I can!" I volunteered fast. *After all*, I thought, *what's a few years' difference when you're in love?* (Of course, Paul, I'll always be true to you. Sort of.)

"Good," he said, "I'll look forward to it. Elizabeth, write, yes?"

"Yes, I will," she said.

The beautiful man drove away, and we all sighed.

"Know what?" M.N. asked.

"What?" said Elizabeth.

"This whole thing could have been a disaster," M.N. said. "I mean, suppose Lisa had gone round the bend anyway? Suppose she had reached a point beyond help."

"She didn't, though," Elizabeth said.

"I know," M.N. answered, "But just suppose."

It was the one thought none of us needed to think. "Now what?" I asked.

"Who knows?" Elizabeth said. "It's Maine for me."

"You are *so* lucky," I said. And then I remembered that with Lisa gone for a while, and Elizabeth away and M.N. beyond the reach of anything but the telephone, I would be alone. I started to cry, and I put my arms around both girls. "What am *I* going to do all summer? I'll be alone!"

"You're behaving like a ten-year-old when camp breaks up," Elizabeth said sharply.

"Exactly," M.N. agreed. "Remember, you've got Brian all to yourself, at last."

That was ridiculous, and I said so. But on the way home, I started to think about it. My Joanne Woodward *had* been successful beyond the dreams of even my shy-er self. Maybe I could try something else, something a little more drastic, a little more advanced, on Brian now. I reached back in my mind, and came up again with Paula Prentiss's voice—deep, musky, seductive, with humor and a sense of *breathless* excitement. I had only used it once before, and that hadn't been a really fair test since it was clutch-playing. Who knew what would happen if I had warm-up time?

Inspirational
Writing for
Young Adults

THEY CAGE THE ANIMALS AT NIGHT
BY JENNINGS MICHAEL BURCH
This poignant childhood memoir recounts
the triumphant tale of a little boy who,
abandoned by his mother at the age of
eight, finally gained the courage to reach
out for love and found it waiting for him.

A LITTLE PRINCESS
BY FRANCES HODGSON BURNETT
The classic story of a little girl, orphaned
while attending boarding school in
England, who learns to face misfortune
and hardship with an irrepressible humor
and undying hope.

Available wherever books are sold or at
signetclassics.com